WHITE POLES

WHITE POLES

by

SHIRLEY FAULKNER-HORNE

Illustrated by
PETER BIEGEL

LONDON
H. F. & G. WITHERBY LTD.
1954

First published in 1954 by
H. F. & G. WITHERBY LTD.
5 Warwick Court, London, W.C.2

MADE AND PRINTED IN GREAT BRITAIN BY PURNELL AND SONS, LTD.
PAULTON (SOMERSET) AND LONDON

To

MY DAUGHTER

ANTHIA

CONTENTS

I wish to thank Mr. P. E. Blackmore for the help he has given me with this book.

CHAPTER ONE

JENNIFER wriggled her toes and finding the hot-water bottle stone-cold and flabby like a codfish, kicked it unceremoniously out of the bed. She yawned and snuggled down again, revelling in the lovely golden glow that comes between sleep and wakefulness; even the little pink clouds scurrying along seemed to be leading nearer and nearer to the land where dreams come true, where she was riding a beautiful pony, and sailing effortless over the fences at the International Horse Show.

There was a shout far below, and the strident clang of the milk lorry as it shuddered to a stop at the farm gates snatched her from the land of nod into the land of reality with a bump. She yawned again, stretched and then suddenly realising what day it was, jumped out of bed. September 20th. Her birthday, her fourteenth birthday! She pulled back the flowered chintz curtains with a flourish and let the sunlight flood into her room.

Jennifer Charrington was a small child with enormous blue eyes, pointed chin, a firm mouth, and an unruly head of fiery red curls. "You only have to look at her to know she's a one, and a determined one at that," remarked Mrs. Long, the daily, with a sad shake of her head. It was her standard remark. Jennifer was not really a naughty child, but she liked her own way and would go to any lengths to achieve it. Provided things

were explained to her logically she could be led any-
where, but pushed never; it was one of the banes of her
existence that grown-ups never bothered to explain
things or give sensible reasons for the rules and regula-
tions they imposed.

Her parents were fairly strict, and as she was an only
child she felt she had an undue amount of discipline;
she forgot of course the undue amount of spoiling.

School did not begin until the 21st, so she had the
whole day to call her own, and as she was the birthday
girl it promised to be a glorious one.

Humming a little tune, she flung her clothes on, then
sped along to her parents' room. She knocked very
softly and waited. Only her father's snores filled the
air—he must be lying on his back. Jennifer knocked
again, a little louder this time, and pressed her ear to
the key-hole.

"Come in," whispered a sleepy voice.

"Good morning, Mummy darling," she said as she
bent down and kissed her.

Her mother, blinking furiously, half-raised herself
in bed. "G-good morning, darling, and many happy
returns."

"Shall I draw the curtains?"

"Yes, do," said Mrs. Charrington, who once she was
awake was fully in possession of all her senses. "It will
help to bring your father gently to a conscious state!
Oh, what a lovely day," she muttered as she leaned over
to the other bed and prodded her husband, who
promptly turned over with something between a snort
and a grunt. "Impossible—he probably thinks it's the
middle of the night and I've got up to stop him snoring."
She winked at Jennifer. "Put the kettle on, darling—

the hissing noise usually does the trick. By the way, if you open the cupboard door you will find something there for you."

This was the moment Jennifer adored most, the moment when she saw the parcel all covered with brown paper and string. It was oblong and had an important-looking label on it. She lifted it carefully and started struggling with the knot. "Ouch, it's terribly tight. Where are the scissors?"

"On the dressing-table."

Jennifer peered amongst the mysterious bottles, brushes and scent sprays that covered the plate-glass top. "I can't see them."

"Well, they were there last night. Let me think. Gordon?"

"Hmm."

"Have you seen my scissors?"

"Hm, what?"

"My scissors. Have you seen my scissors?"

Mr. Charrington rolled over. "Many happy returns, darling. Come and kiss your old man. No—no, a bigger one than that. Now what were you saying, my dear?" He turned to his wife.

Very slowly she repeated, "Have you seen my scissors?"

"Scissors." he muttered, " Let me see."

Oh, this was too much. Why should they decide on their elusive tricks, a complaint all scissors seem to have in common, on this morning of all mornings?

"They're in the bathroom—I took them in there last night to cut my finger-nails."

Jennifer found them balancing precariously on the window ledge.

Snip, snip—the string fell apart, then the paper with its thrilling crackling sound. Inside was a white box which she stroked fondly, finding the final moment of anticipation sweet. She lifted the lid and there, between the folds of tissue paper, lay a pale blue twin set and a Donegal tweed skirt. Jennifer liked clothes, so she was not disappointed by the usefulness of the present; on the contrary, she was rather pleased—it was very grown-up and smart.

Her father, now thoroughly awake after his cup of tea, leaned over and drew from under the bed a chunky, square parcel. "This is from me, darling, with lots of love." He doted on his daughter, and as she bent intently over the package he watched her expression change from one of concentration to one of sheer delight as she saw the little cream wireless set.

"Oh, Daddy, Daddy, how perfectly wonderful!"

"Good, I'm glad you like it—it's for your room, provided you don't keep it on until all hours of the night. Well, run along now while we get dressed. I've taken the day off from the office. I enjoy birthday parties too."

Mr. Charrington, one of the directors of the Camhill Aircraft Company, in Thaxted, had taken to farming as a side-line just after the war. The farm adjoining their house and grounds had come up for sale, so after much thought and consideration he had made the great decision and had never regretted it, for he now derived most of his pleasure from his pedigree herd of Jerseys. He had an excellent manager, and Mrs. Charrington took a great pride and interest in the herd books and all the records.

Moreover, Vanessa Charrington enjoyed the country life, having been born and bred in Eastly, only twenty

miles distant from their present farm. The lovely old
Manor House of her childhood, which had belonged
to her family for generations, had been well cared for
in those days, but now there were only Alice the cook
and old James the butler left to look after the place.
But her mother, Lady Peebles, refused to move.

She was a stubborn old lady and was heard to remark
that the only way she would leave the family house was
when she was carried out feet first. No amount of
persuasion would alter her decision, so her daughter
had given up the unequal struggle. It was sad to see
the grounds gradually deteriorating; and the stables,
long since deserted, were in a crumbling state of dis-
repair. They had been deserted for a long time, for two
years before the war her father, Sir Edward Peebles,
had sold the horses after John, his only son, had died
following a broken back on the hunting field. Mrs.
Charrington had not missed the horses, for ever since
Gipsy, the little bay pony, had bolted with her out
hunting she was scared stiff and every ride was a nightmare to her.

Lady Peebles had been a wonderful horsewoman;
and although she was heartbroken about her son, gossip
had it that she was more upset when the horses were
sold. That was not true, but the story still persisted.
Sir Edward Peebles never rode again and forbade his
wife to go near a horse. When he died in 1950 the old
lady found that the gap was too long to start anew;
and as she was then sixty-seven, and with more than
a touch of arthritis, she decided to rest on her laurels.

Jennifer placed the wireless set on the table beside her
bed and plugged it in. That was like Daddy: he had the
right plug fitted straight away. When June Brentwood,

her best friend, had been given her set they had sent it without a plug at all, and she had to wait hours and haul it down to the local electrician's shop in the village before she could play it.

They had settled down to breakfast when the postman arrived. Most of the mail was for her—birthday cards and one or two packages from godparents and various aunts, a fountain-pen, a Reeves Student paint box, a few books and a large box of chocolates.

"Well," said her father as he drained the last drop of the coffee-pot, "I'm just going for a walk round the farm and have a word with Evans, then we will go out in the car."

"Where, Daddy?"

"Ah, that's a secret. You wait and see. Like to come with me now?"

"Yes," replied Jennifer, who adored animals and the farm.

The cow-shed was having its extra weekly clean, for Mr. Charrington was proud of the model buildings and liked to see them always as clean as a new pin. This caused a certain amount of muttering among the farm workers, but at heart they too were proud of the place and its high standard of efficiency and cleanliness. Her father, finding Evans in the dairy checking the day's records, started to discuss the calving programme for the winter milk production. Jennifer left him to it and wandered over to the home pastures, which sloped down to a softly flowing river. These water-meadows were wonderful for the cattle, and they looked very well and contented. As she leaned over the gate Dolly, her old grey pony, came up in search of a sugar lump. Jennifer had not failed her, for her pockets were bulging with it as this was a birthday morning, a celebration day in which all should share. Dolly was twenty years old, 13-2, and as quiet and reliable as it was possible to find. She never did anything, and as she believed in taking life easily, she had to be literally kicked along. Jennifer naturally adored her, as Dolly had taught her to ride, but she really was rather dull now. Still, in view of the family history and her parents' extreme nervousness, she was lucky to have a pony at all, as they were at pains to remind her. Her mother was still very frightened of horses and seemed scared if Dolly so much as shook her head or laid back her ears, and her father quite simply did not know one end of a horse from another and cared less. Granny Peebles was different, but as she no longer rode, it was not much help. She was allowed the free run of the library at the manor, however, and as the shelves were full of horse books she had absorbed quite a lot from the written words.

All the same, it would be wonderful to have a pony with a bit of life in it, one that could jump, particularly as Jenkins, their new cowman, had spent part of his life in a cavalry regiment and knew a lot about horses. He had actually competed and won the N.C.O.s' jumping at the Delhi Horse Show. The photograph of him receiving the blue rosette had pride of place over the mantelshelf in his cottage.

"Jennifer, Jennifer." It was her father calling, so she ran back to the yard to join him. "I'm just going to get the car out. You run in and get ready and tell Mummy I'll be about five minutes."

She wondered where they could be going; it was rather tantalising, but that was the fun of birthday surprises.

They turned left out of the drive away from the village and in the direction of Eastly. "Oh," cried Jennifer, "I know—we're going to see Granny." Lady Peebles was sure to have something nice for her, and she loved the old mellow rambling house. This was going to be fun!

James opened the door, as impeccable as ever: although times had changed, James had not. He bowed. "Her ladyship is in the drawing-room." As this was the only downstairs room in constant use nowadays, it was not surprising. But James always said it as if she might be in any one of a dozen different places.

Lady Peebles rose as they entered the room. "Good morning, Gordon. Good morning, Vanessa. And Jennifer, darling, many happy returns." She bent to kiss her granddaughter's upturned face. Although the arthritis had caused a slight stoop, she was a very distinguished woman, with a fine-boned face, a firm mouth, piercing eyes and beautiful white hair that was always well-dressed. The portrait that hung above the fireplace showed that the years had not been too unkind; except for a few lines, and the change in the colour of the hair from red to white, it might have been the same person. Jennifer was very much like her; and as the sight of her often brought back memories of her own youth, her granddaughter was a great favourite of hers, and their mutual love of horses drew them very close together.

"Well, as I know you are dying to see what I've got for you"—she slipped on a loose-fitting jacket—"there's no point in delaying, so follow me."

They went out of the french windows, and as they walked slowly along the stone-flagged terrace her grandmother kept pointing her stick at the various clumps of chrysanthemums; she knew them all by name and was proud of the size of the blooms.

It was getting more mysterious every minute. Through the wrought-iron gate and up the rose walk, and then through the green wooden gate in the brick wall and so on into the stable yard.

"Could it be . . .?" Jennifer paused and glanced at her grandmother, whose face was quite expressionless. *Click, click*, went her black cane on the cobblestones as she moved across to the far end of the yard.

A head appeared over the door of the last box, a brown head with a little white star; and as they approached, Willis, the gardener, opened the stable door and led the pony into the yard.

"Jennifer, this is Skipper. How do you like him?"

"You mean . . .?"

"Yes, he's yours," replied Lady Peebles as the child hesitated for a second.

"How do I like him? Oh, Granny, Granny!" She flung her arms round the old lady's neck.

Skipper was a grand sort of pony, with a good shoulder, a short back and plenty of bone. He had a nice small head and his eyes were wide apart, clear and steady. He was dark-brown, had two white socks and stood 14-1. He was everything she had ever dreamed of; he was wonderful. She pinched herself to make sure that it was not a dream, that this pony was really hers. She patted the shining neck, and the pony nuzzled her gently. They were going to get on well together.

"Would you like to have a ride on him?"

"I'd love to, but"—her face fell dejectedly—"I haven't any riding clothes with me."

B

"Yes, you have. I put them in the boot of the car," said her mother.

"While you're changing, Willis will get the pony ready for you and bring him round. Then you can ride in the park and I can watch from the terrace." Jennifer needed no second bidding—she flew back to the car.

Skipper proved a grand ride. Although he never put a foot wrong and moved beautifully, she could feel the courage there, the eagerness. Finally she pulled up below the stone wall of the terrace.

"How do you like him?"

Jennifer patted his neck and the sparkle in her eyes was a good enough answer for her grandmother. "He's marvellous, Granny, absolutely marvellous," she replied.

CHAPTER TWO

JENNIFER went to a day-school, so she was able to ride Skipper every weekend; and as the evenings were light until after five, she managed to get in an hour before dark. She rode mostly round the farm, which consisted of both pasture, arable and woodland, and extended to over four hundred acres. As soon as she began to feel really at home on her pony, she decided to see whether he could jump, so one Saturday, in mid-October, she rode down the long green lane into Bracken Wood, where there were one or two ditches and tree-trunks which would provide low, natural obstacles. Knowing that she was not very expert herself, she had slipped on a neck strap, so that whatever happened she could grab hold of that as they were going over and avoid jobbing the pony in the mouth.

Coming to a small log about a foot high, Jennifer walked up to it, dropped her hands, and Skipper walked over. So far, so good—now she would repeat the performance at the trot, trying to remember to let her body follow the movement of the horse. Skipper trotted over, but Jennifer knew that she had let her weight come forward too early and so lost impulsion at the moment of take-off. She tried again and felt it was much better. Feeling more daring, she cantered slowly down to the tree-trunk that had fallen across the track during the gales in March: it was not very

big, about two feet at the low end and three feet at the
other. Still, Jennifer felt her heart creeping up into her
mouth as they approached it. What would he do?
Skipper pricked his ears, lowered his head and stretched
his neck; Jennifer gripped the neck strap. He took off
like a bird and they both landed safely on the other
side. He jumped so smoothly that Jennifer found she

had hardly moved in the saddle. She felt terribly
excited. Skipper could jump, she owned a pony that
could jump!

Her parents, she knew, would be horrified if she even
breathed the word, so the less said about it, for the time
being, anyway, the better.

Jenkins had watched her progress with interest. She
was improving very rapidly, and if keenness was any

guide she should make a first-class horsewoman. One Saturday, after he had finished the dairy work, he wandered across to the home paddock. It had poured with rain earlier in the day, and as it looked very grey and overcast Mrs. Charrington had only allowed Jennifer to ride provided she kept near the yard. It wasn't much fun in the field; in fact, it was boring.

"Sit up, Miss; you look like a sack of potatoes." She turned to see Jenkins leaning over the gate.

"I know. I'm bored," said Jennifer. "I wanted to go for a ride."

"Now you've got used to the pony it's time you did a bit o' work in the field—a bit of schooling, as you might say."

"I'd love to, but I don't know what to do, and when I am doing anything, whether it's right or not. I wish you'd teach me."

Jenkins' weatherbeaten face lit up; this was what he had been waiting for. He climbed nimbly over the gate.

"Let's see now." He checked her saddle and bridle and then, taking up a position in the centre of the field, he asked her to walk round him in a large circle.

She sat well forward and down in the saddle. He was pleased to see that she had the pony collected and between her hands and legs.

"Trot on," he roared.

Jennifer nearly jumped out of her skin. She had no idea he had a voice like that—it was in the best tradition of the parade-ground. She kicked Skipper hard and he literally leapt forward.

"Right. Pull up," he called. "It may 'ave been me voice that frightened you," he grinned, "but you'd better not be kicking this pony as if it was old Dolly.

'E's got courage and 'as been well schooled. All you want to do with 'im is to give 'im a gentle squeeze just behind the girth. Shorten your reins a little before you begin to trot, and then, at the moment of asking 'im to go on, give a little with your 'ands—see what I mean? So many people kicks them in the guts and takes 'old of the mouth at the same time, asking 'im to stop and go at the same instant, so to speak. Do you know what this language, as you might say, is called?"

"The aids," replied Jennifer.

Jenkins nodded. "How many are there?"

Jennifer had just read about this, so she felt on fairly safe ground. "Four. The legs, the hands, the weight of the body and the voice. These are called the natural aids, and the artificial aids are: spurs, the stick, the martingale——"

"Yes, very good. The legs stimulate impulsion and control the 'ind-quarters, and the 'ands control the fore'and and guide and check the pace." He continued to explain a little about balance and collection. How a horse is considered balanced when he can move himself with maximum ease and efficiency. He considered Skipper had been well schooled, for he was balanced and had a supple back with plenty of power behind the saddle.

Jennifer was absorbed, and the morning passed like a flash.

"Oh, by the way, darling," said her mother at lunch-time, "June Brentwood rang up and asked you for the weekend. As Daddy and I have to go out tonight, and the Maidments are coming to lunch tomorrow, I thought it would be nice for you, so I accepted."

"Oh, good," said Jennifer. "It should be fun." June was one of her best friends. They went to the same school and had the same interest in horses. "Who will look after Skipper, though? It's Jenkins' weekend off."

"Oh, one of the men. I'll get Evans to arrange it," said her father.

"Will he be all right?"

"Of course he will. You're getting as bad about that pony as old Mrs. Snodgrass is about those spaniels of hers."

Jennifer made a face. "Oh, Daddy! Still, you won't forget to tell him that Skipper gets a small feed twice a day now the weather is getting colder and——"

"All right, darling, they'll know—you needn't go into details. Now, if you're ready by two o'clock I'll run you over to June's, as I've got to go into Thaxted again to check on one or two things. It's not far out of my way and will give your mother a chance to rest, too, before this evening."

Mrs. Charrington smiled; it was very thoughtful of her husband. The Grange was a big house to run, with only one living-in servant and a succession of dailies.

Major and Mrs. Brentwood, June's parents, also had a farm, but a smaller unit than the Charrington's— about two hundred and fifty acres. All the family, mother, father and three children, rode; and as Major Brentwood did a little showing and buying and selling as a side-line, the place was full of horses and ponies. They were keen followers of the local pack, and Jennifer had always been envious of the fact that June, her elder brother James, and younger sister Marigold were allowed to hunt. She was even more so now that she had a new pony that would carry her and carry her well.

Major Brentwood was very full of the fact that he had just bought a bay pony that could jump like a stag. It had won quite a bit in the show-ring, but had turned nappy. He felt confident he would be able to cure that and so have a first-class pony for June for the shows next year. The family seemed able to talk of little else, and not long after her arrival Jennifer was dragged out to admire it. It was a nice enough pony, but not half as nice as Skipper; it did not look in the same class, even to her amateur eye. Still, it must be a superb performer to create such an impression in the household. Lucky, lucky June. How she would love to jump Skipper in a show!

After tea they went into Thaxted to the cinema, and as Sunday was wet and cold they spent the day down in the big playroom. June and Marigold were very keen on puppets and were trying to get up a play for Christmas. June was clever with her hands and had made a theatre out of an old orange-box and curtains out of scraps in her mother's sewing-basket. The three of them spent most of the day making scenes for the set and painting them.

Her father was late in collecting her, and as it was pouring with rain she did not go down to see Skipper that night.

While she was getting dressed for school the next morning she heard quite a commotion going on downstairs, so pulling her gym tunic over her head, she ran down to see what it was all about. She froze to a standstill on the last step. Evans, looking extremely agitated, was saying: "Yes, Mr. Boyle, it's the new pony. Can you get over right away?"

Jennifer grabbed his arm. "That was the vet you were talking to. What's happened to Skipper? What is it?"

"I'm not sure, Miss."

"What do you mean, you're not sure? Has he cut himself? Has he?"

"No, Miss. We think it's something he's eaten."

"Something he's eaten. What did he have while I was away?"

"The same as usual, Miss, but we were short-handed and the new boy brought him in to feed and then turned him out into the small paddock, because he thought there was more grass there—the one with the oak tree in it. We think he must have eaten some acorns."

Jennifer looked panic-stricken. "Oh, Evans, will it kill him?"

"No, I don't think it's as bad as that, Miss. I think we have caught it in time. The vet is on his way over."

Mr. Boyle was a dependable man and, true to his word, he pulled up in the yard in less than ten minutes. He looked at Skipper and shook his head.

"What is it?" asked Jennifer fearfully.

"He's had a few acorns, without a doubt."

"Oh, Mr. Boyle, you don't think——" Jennifer looked up at him with an agonized expression.

"No, I think we may have got it in time. I'm going to give him something now, that I think will make him better. Have you a rug?" Jennifer nodded dumbly. "Right. Will you get that on him while I get an injection ready?"

Jenkins, who had returned that morning from his weekend off, had noticed the pony and already had a box prepared for him. Taking over from the trembling Jennifer, he led him in. "There, little one, steady, steady." Skipper, his head down, followed quietly along.

Mr. Boyle appeared with a large glass tray, several needles and small bottles. "I'll give him a purgative and then an injection that will help to counteract the poison."

"Poison!" gasped Jennifer. "He hasn't been poisoned as well?"

Mr. Boyle smiled. "No, but acorns are a form of poisoning, you know."

"Now watch him carefully, and if he starts looking round at his flanks a lot and kicking, let me know at once."

Jennifer was in much too nervous a state to be sent to school, so her parents decided wisely that until Skipper had passed the crisis she had better remain at home.

Jennifer spent the morning with her head over the door of the box. "Oh, Skipper, Skipper," she moaned, "if anything should happen to you I think I'd die."

"Now come, Miss, that's no way for a young girl to be talking," said Jenkins briskly. "The pony will be all right."

"How do you know?"

"Well, I believe in looking on the bright side. It's a mild attack, I'm sure, and we got Mr. Boyle pretty quick."

"Thanks to you," said Jennifer.

"That's as may be, Miss. Now don't go saying anything to Dan, 'e's 'ad 'is telling off, and believe me, 'e'll never do anything so stupid again. 'E will remember to ask first."

"Right, Jenkins, I won't."

"One o'clock, Miss. Now, you can't do any good just standing there. You go up to the 'ouse and get some food. The vet'll be 'ere later on, and then we may know a bit more. I'll stay and keep an eye on 'im."

The time crawled by, every minute like an hour. At last the vet arrived and, going into the box, patted Skipper, who turned his head and looked at him. "Ah, that's better. He's taking a bit more notice of things now. The purgative has worked, too. Watch him tonight and I'll look in tomorrow; and don't forget, if he seems any worse and you are at all worried, call me at once."

"Is he going to be all right?" gasped Jennifer.

Mr. Boyle was cautious. "Well, he's going along well—I'll be able to tell you a little more tomorrow, but I think we got it in time."

That night Jennifer slept very little and kept creeping down to the yard to look at the pony. Finally, at six o'clock, she decided to stay there altogether. She felt happier where she could see him all the time. No amount of pleading would move her until Jenkins, having finished the milking, promised to remain with him.

"Now, you're to eat all that up," said her mother as she placed a large dish of bacon and eggs in front of her.

"I couldn't," replied Jennifer, pushing the plate away from her listlessly.

"Of course you could. It's no good making yourself ill, too. That won't help the pony or anyone else, for that matter. Anyway, Jenkins tells me he is better and thinks that he is out of the wood now."

"We won't know till the vet comes."

"Well, he telephoned while you were sitting in the stable to say he would be along about midday. So you'll know then, I expect."

Mr. Boyle appeared on the stroke of twelve and his heart went out to the child when he saw her pinched white face. He spoke for a few minutes with Jenkins before going in to examine the pony. After what seemed hours he looked up with a smile.

"Well, young lady, I think the pony is going to be all right."

"There now, Miss," put in Jenkins, "what did I tell you?"

"You really do, Mr. Boyle?"

"I do."

"Oh, thank you, thank you."

"Now, Miss," said Jenkins firmly, "you go on up to the 'ouse and get yourself a warm drink and some sleep."

"Taking over, Jenkins?" queried the vet.

"Yes, sir. Go on now, Miss. I'll look after the pony. E's going to be fine."

CHAPTER THREE

SKIPPER recovered quite rapidly, and was hacking about the farm in less than no time. As November progressed and June talked more and more about hunting, Jennifer resolved to sound her parents on the subject. The two months she had had Skipper he had never done a thing wrong, which should prove quite conclusively to them that he was perfectly safe. She decided to ask her father first, for although he knew nothing about horses he was not prejudiced against them or frightened of them like her mother.

The moment came one evening in late November. Her father returned early, and as the front door swung open the house was filled with the strains of "Some Enchanted Evening". The fact that he could not sing a note in tune never daunted Mr. Charrington. When he felt happy he burst forth regardless of time or place. Jennifer left her homework with relief; she had been sitting, head in hands, for the last ten minutes trying vainly to solve an algebra problem. She hated maths and was habitually bottom of the class.

"Hullo, poppet," he called gaily as she jumped down the stairs two at a time. "Where's Mummy?"

"Here," said Mrs. Charrington. "I was just laying the dinner-table. What's all the excitement about?"

"Ah! You both go into the sitting-room and wait a few seconds. What I have to say requires a right and suitable setting."

Completely mystified, they obeyed his instructions and stood waiting patiently in front of the roaring log fire.

Mr. Charrington entered, pushing the trolley in front of him, on which stood three glasses, a bottle of champagne and two packages. He turned to face them. "The Arrowhead passed the final trials with flying colours and the Government have placed a large order. They are to go into service with the Royal Air Force."

Mrs. Charrington stepped forward, her eyes alight, for this had been her husband's special work and problem and was, therefore, his triumph. "Oh, Gordon, I'm so glad. It's wonderful!"

Jennifer hugged him hard too, for she knew what this meant to her father. There was a loud pop and the cork hit the ceiling. It was a gay carefree sound and the sparkling liquid bubbled and frothed in the wide glasses. Jennifer looked with apprehension at the third one, but instead of the usual orange juice, champagne was poured into that as well; it was to be a real celebration.

They lifted their glasses. "To the Arrowhead," they cried in unison.

"And now," said Mr. Charrington, picking up the packages, "such news deserves a present, and there's one each for my very special girls."

Mrs. Charrington's was a lovely gold compact case, and Jennifer's a small gold brooch in the shape of a hunting whip.

A hunting whip! Surely this was the omen. She would pick the right moment when her mother and father had finished talking.

"Daddy," she whispered tentatively.

"Yes?"

"You like Skipper, don't you?"

"Of course I do, but——"

"You think he's perfectly safe, don't you?"

"Yes."

"Well, then, couldn't I hunt him? June goes out every Saturday and nothing happens to her. It's the Sport of Kings, and——"

Her father laughed. "Racing is the Sport of Kings."

"Well, it's a wonderful sport anyway, and I would give anything to be able to go, and you did give me a hunting-whip brooch, surely that means you want me to hunt," gabbled Jennifer all in one breath.

Mr. Charrington glanced helplessly at his wife.

"No, darling," she said firmly.

"But, Mummy," wailed Jennifer. "Why ever not?"

"Because it's dangerous. You know what happened to Uncle John."

"Oh, Mummy, that was years ago, and there is so much wire about now that there aren't many fences left to jump."

"Quite enough," said Mrs. Charrington, who could never forget that terrible day on Gipsy. "Besides, you have no one to go out with."

"Oh, but I have. Major Brentwood would take me."

"No, Jennifer. Now don't spoil Daddy's evening. You are our only child and we're quite determined about it."

The lovely evening fell to pieces about her, so after dinner she crept up to her room and buried her head in her pillow. It was so unfair that just because her mother was frightened of horses and Uncle John had been killed over sixteen years ago she was not allowed to hunt or jump or do anything. She contemplated approaching her grandmother, but she knew that there was only one answer Lady Peebles could give. She got up and, opening the window, let the cold night air play about her face. Somehow the crisp, clean coldness of it soothed her; and glancing at the night sky, with its galaxy of stars, a feeling of loneliness and sheer insignificance crept over her. Here was space, infinite and awesome. Some of those stars were millions of light years away; some were planets, worlds like this one, only larger. There was no end to it. She paused, trying to imagine what something going on for ever, something that had no end, was like. It was too big to grasp. It made all her hopes and fears diminish; she was nothing, nothing more than a minute speck of dust in a vast dome of eternity. She shut the window and turned to the familiarity of her bedroom, drawing comfort from the everyday things that made up her secure little world.

She kicked off her shoes without undoing the straps. If one ever felt bursting with pride and importance, one glance at the clear night sky would be enough to damp the ego of a dictator. Hitler and Stalin could never have allowed themselves the time to pause and contemplate the universe. Grown-ups seemed to have so little time. Perhaps that was where the human race failed; that as one grew older one became penned in by life's everyday needs, its materialism; that contemplative thought vanished, and with it the simple things of life and of God's teaching. On this solemn thought Jennifer fell asleep.

Christmas arrived with its usual round of parties and pantomimes, and the New Year crept in with snow

c

and ice. As all hunting was cancelled Jennifer did not feel so left out of things during the holidays, particularly as their lake was frozen over and the Grange became the centre of activities. They had ice-hockey matches, races, and one night an ice carnival. Some of the grown-ups brought their cars to the edge of the lake and turned on the headlights, the long pencil beams forming a pattern of silver threads across the shining ice. The brazier stoves at various intervals, and the big bonfire at the far end, glowed and crackled in the cold night air. They fried sausages and bacon, and everyone wondered anew why food cooked in the open always tasted so much better. There was punch for the grown-ups, hot glüh-wein for the older children and hot chocolate for the younger ones. Everyone entered into the spirit of the thing and it was really very funny to see some people staggering about and falling flat on their faces. A few of them were so intent on keeping upright that they looked like stiff tin soldiers who never glanced to right or left and when they tried to stop, frantically waved their arms backwards, like an over-zealous windmill.

The roads were packed hard with snow and ice, so it was quite impossible to exercise Skipper, and as he remained out in the field all the time Jennifer was terrified that he would catch cold and die of pneumonia. Sometimes, on particularly cold nights, she would slip on her trousers and thick coat and creep out just to make certain he was still alive. Of course he was, and looking surprisingly perky too, for the rhododendrons and tall hollies made a wonderful wind-break and snug shelter against the keen north wind. Jenkins assured her at least eight times a day that, as he was going to live out, it was far better for him to be out all the time and in all weathers. Animals got acclimatised to it and were far less likely to catch a chill that way than in a box at night; stables could be draughty and horses were very susceptible to draughts. If it had not been for milk production and keeping the yield up, Jenkins would have preferred the cows to have remained out as well, for he was certain that there would have been less chills amongst the herd.

As the days wore on Jennifer saw that Jenkins was right. The drinking water was kept free of ice, and the ponies—old Dolly, now pensioned off, was in the same field—were fed on good rye grass and clover hay, the last lot being taken out late, so they had something to keep them occupied most of the night. As well as hay, they had a feed twice daily which consisted of two pounds of crushed oats, one pound of carrots cut lengthways, some bran and chaff. The ponies were always fed at the same time and the buckets placed well apart to ensure that they got their full share.

Towards the end of the holidays the local branch of the pony club held its annual children's party at the Eastly Hall, and Jennifer was allowed to go with the Brentwoods. She was very excited because her aunt in America had sent her a lovely pale yellow party-dress for Christmas, and this was the golden opportunity to wear it.

Mrs. Charrington was slightly surprised and not a little amused at all the preparations for the big event, for everything had to be just right. Jennifer twirled in front of the mirror, preening this way and that. "You don't think it dips a little at the back, do you, Mummy? Do you think the bow in my hair would

look better a little more to this side?" She refused to
put on her coat properly in case it creased the dress and
was quite appalled when she found that they had to go all
the way in a Land Rover, as the roads were so bad.

After a good tea the radiogram was turned on for
dancing, and she felt very grown-up and proud, for
James Brentwood, one of the best-looking boys in the
room, danced with her nearly all the time. The evening
ended with a film show, and as the lights dimmed and
the horses flicked on the screen she forgot all about
messing up her dress and flopped eagerly down on the
floor with the others. First there was an instructional
film, and then a short story of a riding holiday across
Exmoor, and finally a thrilling film which included
dressage, cross-country and show-jumping, compiled
by the experts.

Firstly it showed the common faults of the incorrect
seat, followed closely by a detailed analysis of the
correct seat, clearly and concisely explained. The
dressage display was given by Mrs. V. D. S. Williams
on her famous horse Pilgrim; Major Rook on Starlight
showed how a cross-country course should be ridden;
and finally the art of show-jumping was demonstrated
by two of the leading personalities at the game; Colonel
Harry Llewellyn on his immortal Foxhunter and Miss
Pat Smythe on the grey, Tosca, performing at the White
City.

Jennifer was enthralled and fired with enthusiasm.
How wonderful it would be to be able to ride like that!
When the film ended and the lights came on once more,
Jennifer sat staring in front of her, immersed in a
rose-coloured dream where Skipper was sailing over
the fences in that large thrill-packed arena, The White

City! The International Horse Show! The words drummed through her head like a magic refrain.

"Wake up—you can't stay here all night," said James, giving her a playful dig in the ribs.

Jennifer rose slowly to her feet. "Wasn't that film marvellous?"

"Not bad," remarked James, who was basically more interested in football than horses.

"Oh, I thought it was heavenly," Jennifer sighed. "How I'd adore to ride at the White City. Think of——"

"Well, you're not even allowed to ride in the local gymkhanas, so I should cut that little dream right out of your head. Come on, it's time to go home." Jennifer followed obediently.

The thaw came at the end of January, and Jenkins wisely lunged the pony before allowing Jennifer to put a leg across him. As the evenings were lengthening she managed to ride after school, and Jenkins instructed her in the turns and circles. He was quick to perceive that she was really concentrating and so her position in the saddle had greatly improved.

"That's right, walk on," called out a voice from behind.

"Why, Granny, I didn't know you were coming over. How lovely to see you." She rode up to Lady Peebles, who was leaning on her stick watching her.

"Well, I thought it was about time I came over to see how you were getting along. I know Jenkins has been teaching you and I was anxious to see the progress. Go out and give me a show."

Jennifer did as she was bidden. Her grandmother, who had had a great deal of experience, asked her first

of all to walk the pony round in a circle, then round at the ordinary trot and finally at the canter. Jennifer thought she was doing this quite well until Lady Peebles explained to her that if she wanted to be an expert she would have to work a great deal harder and ride her pony into the bit, for at present she was allowing Skipper to do all the work.

She chatted to Jenkins for a few minutes and explained that she thought Jennifer should practise pushing the pony more with her legs, so as to get the hindquarters further underneath him, thus achieving the object of the forward movement with correct head carriage.

"Once more, dear, and use those legs."

Jennifer tried very hard, and twice she managed to get the pony going really well.

"That's much better. Keep it up now."

"I'll try. Granny?"

"Yes, my dear?"

"Skipper can jump."

"Most ponies can," replied Lady Peebles non-committally.

"I mean he jumps very well. I do wish I could hunt or jump him or something—it seems such a waste——"

"Ah, there you are, Vanessa. I've just been watching a most interesting display." She turned once more to her granddaughter. "As it's getting a little chilly I think I'll go along in now."

The moment had passed. Jennifer could have screamed. It was too sickening for words: What was the use of having a wonderful pony if you could not do anything with him but merely hack round the farm? Why had her grandmother bothered to buy him?

He must have cost an awful lot of money. It was going to be a long time before she knew the answers to these questions.

CHAPTER FOUR

ONE Saturday morning at the beginning of March Jennifer decided to go for a long ride—it was a heavenly day, warm and cloudless, with a hint of spring in the air. There was something about those first days of spring, when the earth stirred from its long winter sleep, that made old and young feel glad to be alive. Her father sang lustily in his bath, her mother appeared in her new spring costume, and the farm-workers hummed as they went about their work. Jennifer felt like the young lambs; she wanted to leap and jump for joy; little tingly feelings kept running up and down her spine; she felt tensed and expectant; something wonderful was going to happen. The flowering crocus bulbs made a carpet of royal purple and gold beneath the chestnut trees at the bottom of the lawn, a few early primroses peeped out shyly from the mossy bank and the air was filled with the song of birds.

Armed with a halter, Jennifer walked out to the home paddock. She called, rattled the bucket, and Skipper, with a carefree toss of his head, came trotting across the field towards her. He looked gay and light-hearted too. They were going to have a grand ride.

Bracken Wood was the first port of call, for it was her secret place and, unknown to anyone, she had made some jumps by dragging gorse and small branches across the ride. One was over three feet six inches high, and by putting a small gorse bush in front of the ditch she had managed to make quite a spread. Skipper took them all at a nice easy pace, faultlessly and effortlessly. He seemed to know quite a lot about the game and really to enjoy it. Although Jennifer adored jumping and was beginning to feel at one with her pony, she was wise enough not to carry on too long so that he would get bored and sick of it—twice round if he jumped well and finish was her programme.

She patted him. "Good boy, you really do jump superbly." She slipped from the saddle and gave him a lump of sugar.

It was really a heavenly day, and as the sun was quite warm she walked to a nearby tree-trunk, taking the reins over Skipper's head as she went, and sat down on the grass. The pony nibbled the young grass shoots and Jennifer, pulling a rather crumpled packet of biscuits out of her pocket, munched idly away.

Skipper heard it first. His head shot up and he stood quivering with excitement.

"What is it, old boy?"

He snorted and pawed the ground by way of an answer. Jennifer glanced around. There was nothing in sight, and then, borne on the soft spring breeze, she heard it too; the full-throated voice of hounds. She mounted swiftly and remained standing perfectly still on the edge of the cover, her one concern being not to head the fox. Skipper tossed his head and began to fidget, champing the bit in his mouth. "Steady," she whispered, rubbing her hand soothingly up and down his neck—the slightest sound might turn the fox.

A few seconds later she saw, about three hundred yards in front of her, a red streak flash out of the wood and go away over the lower pastures in the direction of Rigby Firs. Hounds followed some distance behind, their noses pressed to the earth and their sterns high. Then Jennifer heard the long note of the horn. It stirred something in her; she felt the blood racing in her veins, and a strange excitement filled her. Hunting! The word that had held magic for generations of Peebles burst upon her with all its force; she would follow, she had to follow, the choice was no longer hers.

She watched the people go by and then followed on well behind them. Suddenly she felt the pony give a little jump on the air, and before she realised what was happening she was galloping forward at a terrific pace, racing past the field. She tried to stop, but the more she pulled the faster went the pony and she became

really frightened. What on earth could she do? She
seized one rein and, tugging hard with both hands,
managed to pull round; and once she was facing in the
opposite direction she found she could stop.

"Whew!" gasped Jennifer. "Skipper, you naughty
pony, how could you?"

As she stood trying to recover her breath something
Jenkins had said crept back into her mind. "Never
take a dead pull at a pony, Miss, you'll never stop 'em
that way. Just give and take a little, so to speak."

After a few minutes she turned round and saw to her
amazement that quite a few horses were standing still
outside the nearby covert. They had not gone so far
away after all. The desire to follow once more crept
over her and so, shortening the reins, she walked forward cautiously. Everyone was very silent, their heads
tilted slightly to one side as they listened to hounds.

She pulled up behind them, feeling Skipper quivering
and shaking beneath her. She felt rather like that herself when suddenly there was a holloa from the other side
of the covert.

The field moved off down the wide ride that ran
through the centre of the wood and Jennifer, keeping
well to the rear, followed at a slow canter. They pulled
up again as they came to the edge of the wood and
Jennifer realised that, instead of a check, they were
waiting their turn to jump.

"Go on, little lady, it's your turn," said a voice
beside her.

She looked up startled and realised that the man in
the pink coat was addressing her.

It was a small rail, but even so she went at it nervously, not quite knowing what would happen. Skipper

pricked his ears, and before she had time to realise it
they were over and galloping on after the others. She
felt more in control of the pony now and less as if she
was being run away with. In fact, as she remembered
Jenkins' advice, she tried to pull up and Skipper slowed
to a hand canter. Jennifer grinned. It worked! Now
it was going to be fun. Over a ditch and on again with
the turf flying beneath her, the wind in her face, and
the smell of hot horses in her nostrils. This was what
being alive really meant.

They checked again at the bottom of Samson's Hollow
and Jennifer was glad of the breather. She kept away
from the rest of the field again in case anyone should
ask awkward questions. It was luck indeed that the
Brentwood family were away for the weekend.

Hounds cast about for several minutes and Jennifer
was fascinated as she watched them trying to work out
their line. They came towards her, weaving up and
down, and she prayed that Skipper would not let out
at one of them—it was a terrible disgrace to kick hounds.
The pony twitched his tail and laid back his ears—a
big black-and-tan hound was just behind him. She
played with the bit frantically and managed to take his
mind off it. The moment passed and Jennifer breathed
a sigh of relief.

A hound spoke, then another and another; they
were on the line again and the field moved off, down a
really steep hill and over a wide deep ditch at the
bottom. The take-off was rather slippery and Jennifer's
heart flew into her mouth as the big grey in front of her
slipped, lunged and dropped his hind legs into it.
However, like most ponies, Skipper was clever and
cat-like, and somehow managed to scramble across

with Jennifer clinging round his neck. Climbing back
into the saddle, she galloped on up the hill, finding
the going much lighter as they left the valley behind.
The melting snow and the heavy February rain had
completely waterlogged the land, and the mud in
places, especially near the farm tracks, was terrible.

They trotted up Honey Lane and through the big
iron gates into Redman Park, where Jennifer was
surprised to see the field split up, most of them going
off to the right. She paused for a second. Which way
should she go? Perhaps it would be nicer and safer to
get out of the crowd. She turned to the left.

The springy turf of the well-drained park-land felt
wonderfully smooth beneath her, and as she stood up
in the stirrups and rested her hands on the wither she
noticed the cows beneath the fine old oak tree look up
and gaze nonchalantly at the weird capers of man.
As they neared the end of the park she saw that the
small group had checked and were standing around
while the whip struggled with a wired-up rail over a
small gate.

"It seems fixed to me. Can't shift it no'ow," he
remarked gloomily.

"Well, that settles it, Hawkins, we'll have to jump
it. Come on, I'll give that old horse of yours a lead."
The man in rat-catcher sailed over, followed by the
whip, who was muttering something unprintable about
wire.

Jennifer glanced about her. Good gracious, where
had everyone disappeared to? Instead of half a dozen
or more, there were only two men left.

"Can your pony jump?" queried one of them.

"I think so," she muttered nervously.

"Would you like to have a go then?"

There did not seem to be any other alternative, and as hounds were running she took her courage in both hands and replied boldly, "Yes, I'll try."

"Good girl. Take it steady now."

She turned Skipper round and approached the fence straight; then, clutching the neck strap, she squeezed the pony, dropped her hands and closed her eyes. Up and over. Although she lost a stirrup and finished up nearer the pony's ears than the saddle, she did not come off.

"That's a good pony of yours. You ought to jump him in some of the shows," said the taller of the two men as he galloped past.

They could still hear hounds faintly in the distance and then suddenly all was silent. In front, the whip pulled up and the others followed suit.

"They're either running mute or they've lost him," said one of the men.

They stood still, listening intently, and the minutes dragged slowly by.

"They're down in Piper's Wood. It sounds as if they've run him to ground."

"By George, I think you're right, Fordingham." They moved off quickly.

Jennifer, noticing that Skipper was sweating pretty hard, decided that this was the moment to head for home. She glanced at her watch and was horrified to see that it was nearly one o'clock. She would be very late for lunch, but anything was worth it, even a row. It had been a wonderful day.

As she patted her pony's neck and loosened the girth she decided that it would be better to tell her parents a little of the morning's activities, even if she failed to mention the fact that they had actually followed and jumped the gate with the rail. What had the man said, something about jumping at the local shows? What a glorious dream, just to be able to compete! If only she was allowed to jump Skipper. If he put up a performance like today's there would be no stopping him!

Suddenly she remembered something—they had called the man Fordingham. Could it be *the* Fordingham, the well-known show-jumping figure? Of course it must be; how foolish of her not to realise that before. He must have come over from the neighbouring county for a day's hunting.

"Skipper, Skipper, do you know he thinks you could show-jump? He said so, he really did. Oh, if only we could!"

CHAPTER FIVE

THE next weekend she managed to persuade her mother to let her ride over and spend the day with June, as she had discovered a way which avoided the main roads. Jenkins too had taken great pains to reassure Mrs. Charrington that the pony was reliable and perfectly quiet in traffic. Jennifer grinned to herself. All this fuss about going for a ride off their own property. What would they have said if they could have seen her last Saturday?

She arrived to find the Brentwoods very busy schooling in the paddock and preparing for the show season. Marigold was on their four-year-old grey, a 13–2 Anglo-Arab, and June was on the new bay, who, after a season's hunting and quiet but firm handling, seemed to have settled down.

Jennifer sat and watched for a while, and then, turning to Major Brentwood with a pleading expression, said: "Couldn't I join in?"

"Why, yes, of course, if you'd like to. Fall in behind Marigold, but don't get too close to her pony's heels, you might get kicked; and go carefully. We don't want any accidents with you, my dear, do we?"

Everyone treated her as if she was a piece of Dresden china. She was getting terribly sick of it and wished that her family would grow up and stop making such a fuss. It made her feel ridiculous in front of the other children.

Major Brentwood was quite amazed with Jennifer's performance: she was quick to grasp what he meant, rode competently and used her head. The pony was a topper and most beautifully schooled. It was a pity the child was not allowed to do more with him. He wished, too, that he could really train Jennifer and bring her out. She had a natural aptitude and keenness that far outstripped his own daughters'. He sighed. Life was like that. Here was a child that could go far, prevented from doing so by highly nervous parents; and his own children, who had all the opportunity in the world, did not seem really interested. The fact that they were forced to ride every day, and instead of a pleasure it had become a business, was a great contributory factor to this state of affairs, a point that Major Brentwood had overlooked. As his enthusiasm increased his children's was inclined to decrease.

"Right; that was quite good, all of you. Now, June, I'd like to finish up with a few jumps."

The fences in the main schooling field were good ones and gave a fair sample of what the children were likely to meet in the ring. The poles were white and some of the fences were brightly painted to get the ponies used to odd-looking jumps. There were straight fences such as a gate, a post and rails and a vivid yellow wall; spread fences like a triple bar painted red and white, parallel bars and a hog's back; and lastly, one or two tricky narrow fences such as a stile and a small wicker gate to test the ponies' obedience. These and a few others were moved every time they were jumped, so that neither horse nor rider should get too accustomed to them.

D

Major Brentwood seldom put the schooling fences up, for he was a great believer in not over-facing them. However, as everything had been going quite well he decided to see how the bay would go round a course of regulation height.

June had a jump over a small pole first to get her going.

"Good," said Major Brentwood. "Now I want you to go over the brush, the small hog's back, then the little stile." June nodded. "Next, the gate, then diagonally across to the oxer." Here was the change of rein that had now become such a feature of the average show-jumping course. "Over the double—there is exactly twenty-four feet—one non-jumping stride—between the two lots of white poles, then the triple bar and lastly the wall."

June proceeded to jump quite a good round, only touching the gate and wall behind. The pony seemed inclined to drop its hindlegs a little, but it was a good performance for the first time and Major Brentwood seemed very pleased and warm in his congratulations. He had just finished putting up the fences that had fallen when a bell clanged loudly from the house.

"Oh, dear, that means I'm wanted on the telephone. Just walk the pony about for a few minutes, June, then put her in. We've done enough for today."

Jennifer realised that this was her chance, the golden opportunity to see how Skipper went in cold blood over proper fences. There was no grown-up in sight and June and Marigold were walking round deep in conversation, not paying the slightest attention to her. Unfortunately there was no time to put Skipper over the practice pole; she merely cantered round before approaching a fence and had cleared the first three before her astounded friends gathered what was happening.

"Jennifer, Jennifer," screamed June in terror. "Stop, oh please STOP!"

But Jennifer had no intention of stopping. The frantic shrieks had put Skipper off slightly as he came to the gate, but he put in a quick one and literally screwed over it. Jennifer, whose first experience this was of a real screw with the hindquarters, pitched right over the pony's neck. She pulled up, regained her stirrup and continued on to the oxer, completely deaf to the continuous pleas of her friends. They were really worried, for what would Mr. and Mrs. Charrington say if anything happened to Jennifer when she was spending the day with them? Their anxiety proved groundless, however, for Skipper cleared the last fences beautifully and Jennifer never looked like moving in the saddle again.

"Gosh!" gasped June as she rode up to them. "I—I don't know w-what to say. I d-didn't know you could even jump, but——"

"Well, now you do," answered Jennifer.

"I know, but not like that." June, who was still rather shaken, added, "But supposing anything had happened to you?"

Jennifer whipped round. "And why should it, may I ask? I'm sick of being thought of as a stupid ninny who can't do anything. I *have* jumped before, I *can* jump and ride just as well as you two."

"Better, I think," replied June who, with a quick flash of intuition, realised just how her friend was feeling. "Goodness, he really is a marvellous pony.

I do think it is a shame that you can't put him into one or two shows."

"Whatever was all that yelling about? I dropped the telephone and came flying out. I thought something dreadful had happened."

"It did—I mean, it didn't. Jennifer jumped Skipper,"

bubbled Marigold before anyone could stop her, "and cleared every fence too."

Major Brentwood turned to Jennifer. "Is this true?"

She nodded. "I knew he could jump; and oh, I don't know, I just couldn't resist it."

"I see. And what are your mother and father going to say?"

Jennifer looked up quickly. "Oh, please don't tell them. They'll only worry, and they might stop me riding altogether."

The elder man smiled; he knew how she felt, and if the pony could go round that course faultlessly it must be a top-class pony. Lady Peebles was a wily old lady. "All right. If you promise not to do it again while I'm around here and put me in a difficult position, I won't say a word."

"I promise," said Jennifer as she went off to put Skipper in one of the empty boxes.

The old white-painted door stood open as the children came across the garden to lunch. Mrs. Brentwood believed in fresh air and at every possible opportunity threw open all the doors and windows. The sunshine poured in, touching with an artist's hand the rich colouring of the lovely Persian rug as it lay framed in all its beauty on the golden, gleaming, polished floor. A bowl of daffodils and forsythia stood on the Sheraton table, and in one corner a great copper jug of chestnut buds reached up to touch the Adam fresco. It was a lovely old house, although sadly in want of repair, but the farm and horses had first call on the Brentwood finances, so the house, like an impoverished but proud person, clung to its dignity and memories of bygone, better times.

"June, there's a letter for you," said Marigold as she passed the chest in the hall.

"Oh good, it's my B.S.J.A. membership thing," said June, picking it up and slipping it into her pocket.

"You are lucky," sighed Jennifer. "I wish I could belong to all these things."

"Well, there's no reason why you shouldn't. You don't have to jump to be a juvenile member, and the subscription is ten shillings. Here," said June, "take a look at it—you'll see all about it and where to write and so forth, I expect."

Jennifer grabbed the envelope eagerly. To be a member of the Association, to have a badge, even if she could not jump, would be something. "Juvenile members, ten shillings." June was quite right. "All subscriptions to be sent to the Secretary, B.S.J.A., 43 Russell Square, London." Well, as she would be able to afford that amount out of her savings, she would send the money off on Monday.

"How did the pony jump this morning?" asked Mrs. Brentwood, as she served out the vegetables.

"Fine," replied her husband. "I think we might do something with him this year."

"Good. He isn't Grade J.A. is he?"

"No, he just missed that last year."

"What does Grade J.A. mean?" queried Jennifer as she gulped down a piece of potato.

"Goodness, don't you know that?"

"Now, Marigold, there is no reason why she should. You explain it to her, Norman," put in Edith Brentwood, turning to her husband.

"Well, at shows that are affiliated to the B.S.J.A. they have classes for good ponies and not so good ponies; otherwise, you see, it would not be fair."

"You mean that the good ponies would win every class and the others wouldn't get a look in?" queried Jennifer.

"Precisely—they would never win a prize at all." Major Brentwood took a sip of beer. "So as show-jumping became more and more popular and the ponies and horses better and better, they devised a scheme whereby any horse that had won over one hundred and fifty pounds in prize money went up into the Grade A class and any pony over twenty pounds into Grade J. A. Juvenile A."

"Goodness, that's an awful lot, isn't it?"

He smiled. "Quite a lot, yes. But people with good horses and ponies travel around to all the shows, and as the first prizes are usually——"

"Daddy," interrupted June. "If a pony qualifies for Grade A is it always a Grade A pony?"

"Yes," replied her father, "provided it is registered."

"Registered?" queried June.

"Yes. Say our bay pony had qualified last year, for example. Well, his name and description and the list of all classes he had won would be lodged with the B.S.J.A. under his owner's name. Then when he was sold, I would have to write to the Association, tell them of the purchase and re-register him in my name. When that was completed, the pony could compete in all Grade A classes."

"Major Brentwood, you know the children's jumping at the White City? Is that open to anyone?" asked Jennifer.

"Yes it is, isn't it, Daddy?" put in June quickly. "Didn't you say they had a qualifying competition there?"

Major Brentwood smiled. "That's a qualifying competition for the Championship Cup. No, I'm afraid all the ponies have to be top class. It's a very high standard indeed, you know."

"Yes, I expect it is. Oh dear, I'd love to be able to jump Skipper there," said Jennifer wistfully.

"Well, if he jumped like he did today he'd probably win it," said June stoutly. "It's a pity you can't jump him. It wouldn't be any good us saying anything, would it?"

"No, dear," put in Mrs. Brentwood firmly, "we can't interfere in family matters, it's just not done; and anyway, I expect Mr. and Mrs. Charrington have a very good reason why they don't wish Jennifer to compete." She was a great upholder of authority. "Who'd like to feed the chickens for me and collect the eggs?"

The response was not overwhelming, but as it was one of the chores that had to be done the children decided to get it over quickly. Mrs. Brentwood believed in having the chickens out on free range; the idea of keeping them either in cages or in straw-filled barns appalled her. She did not agree always with the modern methods; her thought for the birds overriding that of commercial advancement. "But the poor things must have sunlight and air," she was heard to exclaim. "Their natural habit is pecking around a field, and the idea of keeping the light on all night just to make them lay more—it's monstrous and downright cruel."

Her husband laughed at her, but for the sake of peace and quiet allowed her to have her own way, for the poultry was her department.

After they had fed the chickens and returned with two baskets full of eggs, they had to set to and wash them. This was a task everyone hated—it was one of Jennifer's duties at home too—but as dirty eggs were naturally not acceptable, and money was deducted for an egg with the slightest stain, it was a very necessary job.

After the task was completed, they played French cricket before Jennifer started on the homeward track. As she walked slowly along the country lanes the buds, purple with expectancy, seemed to be waiting, like an actor for his cue, to burst forth in new green cloaks. She felt the stirring of the earth, that glorious glad awakening that was part of the miracle of spring. This was the time when courage and hope returned to all living creatures, no less to her. She would tackle her parents once again; after all, nothing venture nothing win, and she would brave anything to realise her ambition.

CHAPTER SIX

SUNDAY was a quiet, peaceful day at the Grange, and after church her father would often clamber into an old pair of slacks and potter about the garden. So one Sunday at the end of March Jennifer decided to help him, as it would give her the ideal opportunity to bring up the question of riding and jumping. After all, he was not nervous of horses like her mother, just disinterested; so if she could tackle him first and win him over he could then exert his influence, which was considerable, over her mother.

Scrambling into her brown corduroy slacks and yellow sweater, Jennifer went out in search of her father and found him outside the potting shed.

"Can I help, Daddy?"

"You can, indeed, if you'd like to. I'm just going to re-do these carnations; they look as if they are getting a little pot-bound. Also the chrysanthemums. You'll find some bigger flower-pots in the shed, there on the left."

After fetching and carrying for her father and working in silence for a while, she asked: "Daddy, you're not really nervous now about my riding, are you?"

"No, poppet. Pass me the trowel, will you? It's just behind you."

"I mean, now you know Skipper is so reliable, you wouldn't mind me jumping, would you?"

50

"Well, there's no need to jump, is there? I mean, there are plenty of gates on the farm, so you are not restricted from going around."

"Oh, Daddy," she cried. "That's not the point. I like jumping."

"How do you know if you haven't tried it?"

"I just know," she replied quickly. "After all, everyone learns to jump; in fact, no one considers you can ride at all unless you can—no one at school, anyway."

"I see," replied her father, looking at her quizzically. "What do you want to jump?"

"Oh, just small poles in the field, and gates and things."

"Gates! Good heavens. They're enormous!"

Jennifer laughed. "Not the farm gates, Daddy. I mean fences that are made for jumping, ones that knock down if you hit them. Jenkins would be there all the time and you know he is very good. Oh, Daddy, please, please, say yes. I hate being thought a cissy at school. When the others hear I've got a pony but don't jump they just laugh at me."

That last remark had the desired effect—no one was going to laugh at his daughter. "All right, poppet, I'll have a word with your mother and then, if she agrees, I'll speak to Jenkins."

Jennifer flung her arms round his neck and hugged him.

Mr. Charrington had quite a battle with his wife, but when she was assured that Jennifer would be allowed to jump only low fences that would knock down at the slightest touch, and only when Jenkins was in attendance, she relented. Even so, she could not conquer her nervousness, and every time she knew Jennifer was going over a one-foot pole she would bite her finger-nails to the bone.

Now that Jennifer had her parents' permission to jump in the field she felt she was one step nearer her goal. As the Easter holidays approached, Jenkins spent quite a lot of time, making fences and he was agreeably surprised, not to say astonished, at her performance.

"This ain't the first time you've jumped that pony, is it, Miss?"

Jennifer was non-committal. "Well, you have to go over a log or a ditch sometimes when you're out riding, don't you?"

"You've jumped over more than a log or a ditch, Miss: now be honest."

"All right, Jenkins, I have."

The man grinned. "I thought so. I had call to go to Bracken Wood yesterday after them rabbits."

"Oh, Jenkins, you won't tell, will you, not now I'm allowed to jump? If Mummy thought I'd done it without her permission she might stop me now, she'd be so furious."

"Well, if you keeps your side of the bargain and don't jump up there no more I won't say nothing."

"Oh, thank you, Jenkins."

The man knew a good pony when he saw one, and Skipper was a real one. He fell to wondering where Lady Peebles had found him and what his history was. No one seemed able to throw any light on the problem. Mrs. Charrington said she had no idea, and Mr. Charrington at first could not understand why Jenkins was so persistent. A pony was a pony, wasn't it? However, when Jenkins spoke to him one morning after giving Jennifer a lesson, he resolved to ask his mother-in-law.

"Mind you, sir, I ain't said anything to Miss Jennifer. It wouldn't do for a one like 'er to think that 'e could jump more than just a small fence," put in Jenkins quickly.

Lady Peebles, when approached, merely smiled blandly. "Where did I get the pony, Gordon? Through a friend, of course. How else? After all, I don't know why you should be so surprised. I was always supposed to be a good judge of horse-flesh." She looked up at him with a twinkle. "When I buy one, I buy a good 'un—it doesn't cost any more to keep." Beyond that she refused to go.

Mr. Charrington smiled; she was a stubborn, artful old woman. Anyway, why worry. If his mother-in-law liked to throw her money about on horses, who was

he to complain? His daughter had a good, reliable
pony, one that wasn't likely to let her down—that was
all that mattered, and should make his wife happier, to
say the least of it. With that thought, the subject was
closed as far as he was concerned. It would have been
anything but closed if he could have taken a peep inside
Jennifer's head.

Now that the first obstacle had been accomplished she
felt a great deal happier. After a few lessons with
Jenkins, she thought one of the best forms of diplomacy
for any further scheme was to ask her mother to come
down one morning and watch. Perhaps when she saw
how beautifully Skipper took everything she might
consent to a little more adventurous programme.

Mrs. Charrington was indeed very surprised both at
her daughter's prowess and the pony's style—he never
looked like putting a foot wrong. It seemed harmless
enough too, and Jennifer looked as if she was in her
seventh heaven. Perhaps, after all, she was making a
fuss about nothing; one could not keep one's child per-
manently wrapped in cotton wool. Because she had
been pushed and badgered into riding and hunting
against her will, she had gone to the other extreme with
Jennifer, and protected her against all dangers. Perhaps
she had been wrong.

"That was very good, darling," she said as Jennifer
rode up to her.

"Doesn't he jump superbly, Mummy?"

"Yes, he does."

"Oh, Mummy, when you see the way he jumps and
you know that even if he did make a mistake all that
would happen is the fence would come tumbling down,
you can't be frightened, surely?"

Mrs. Charrington laughed. "Not so much, certainly."

"Mummy, couldn't I jump him at one of the little shows round here? June has gone to one today. After all, the fences there are better made and they all fall down at the slightest touch—sometimes, June says, by the draught made by the horse's tail!"

Mrs. Charrington smiled; she looked so keen and eager, it seemed a shame always to say no. After all, the other kids seemed to do it without trouble. "Well, we'll see. I'll have a talk with Daddy."

"Mummy, Mummy, you absolute angel!"

"I only said I'd talk it over with Daddy. Don't forget we're going over to see Granny this afternoon; she's having a tea-party."

Jennifer felt so happy that she did not mind the idea of a grown-up tea-party. Usually they filled her with horror, for she had to listen to the dreariest conversations, be continually jumping up and down to hand things round, so that she never had time to eat more than one cream cake; and to crown it all, half the people looked at her as if she were something out of a cracker. "But, my dear, how you're grown," or "You are getting a big girl now." What did they expect her to do, remain the size of a pigmy?

As they drove over to the Manor Jennifer sat beside her mother, silently immersed in her thoughts. She might be allowed to jump in a few shows. She would not, however, be able to qualify for the White City, because to win twenty pounds in prize-money would mean that she not only had to be very good, but that she would have to travel round all over the place, and this she knew would be quite impossible. Jennifer sighed. The small shows and gymkhanas would be fun, but there was something about the International that fired her imagination to the point where it became almost an obsession.

The lovely mellow brick of the old Tudor house glowed a dull rose colour in the afternoon sunlight, and as their car came to a stop outside the great oak door the two peacocks screeched a welcome and spread their feathers like a rainbow-coloured fan. The house, nestling in the peaceful hollow away from the bustle

of the outside world, seemed to have changed little through the centuries. What dramas it had witnessed! The defeat of the Armada; the terror of the Cromwellian times, when hunted Jacobites found refuge in its secret places. The gay days of King Charles, and other more sombre moments, when a Peebles left its peaceful boundaries to fight for all it stood for. The solid, comfortable, complacent days of the Victorian era, and then the last forty tremendous years, when wars shook its foundations and the air was filled with the roar of planes.

A jet flew overhead, its attendant scream sounding like the wail of a banshee or the cry of all souls in torment. Now, nowhere was quiet, nowhere was sacred from the hand of machine-mad men. Even Jennifer, a product of the age, felt a queer feeling of regret that the scene of such serenity should have been shattered in one swift moment.

Her grandmother, seated in her Chippendale chair, was deep in conversation with a man in riding clothes when they entered the room.

"Ah, there you are, Vanessa!" She lifted her face for a kiss. "And Jennifer, darling—how are you?"

"Very well, thank you, Granny."

"May I introduce Colonel Saunders. My daughter Vanessa, and my granddaughter."

"How do you do." As Jennifer shook the tall lean man by the hand she hesitated for a second. Surely this was the famous show-jumping figure! She recognised his face from the photographs.

"Are you *the* Colonel Saunders?"

"It depends what you mean by *the* Colonel Saunders," he replied with a twinkle.

Jennifer blushed. "The—the show-jumping one."

"Yes, one and the same."

"Oh," said Jennifer glancing up at him shyly. There were so many things she would like to ask him, so many things she wanted to say, but she felt suddenly tongue-tied and only managed to stammer out: "H-how is Z-Zephyr?"

"He is very well now, thank you. I shall be jumping him again this season, as his leg has quite recovered."

E

"Oh, good, I——"

She did not have time to say anything more to the great man, as two other guests were ushered into the room.

Jennifer knew it was rude to stare, but she found it very hard not to keep looking at Colonel Saunders. She had a photograph of him on his famous Zephyr in her bedroom, and to be actually sitting in the same room with him—it was too wonderful to believe.

She gathered from the subsequent conversation that the Colonel was in the district looking at horses and that he had met her grandmother the previous day. One of his hobbies was collecting old sporting prints, and when he discovered that Lady Peebles had a very fine collection he had accepted her invitation to call and view them.

This was one grown-up tea-party that was anything but boring, and Jennifer nearly dropped her tea-cup when Colonel Saunders enquired about her pony.

She told him about Skipper and how she had started jumping, and then, as he seemed so very interested, she lost her head and blurted out: "He really does jump superbly; he pops over four-foot-six without turning a hair." Jennifer bit her lip. What *had* she said? "I—I mean, I'm sure he could jump that by the way he goes over the little fences."

As she was looking down, playing with her handkerchief, she failed to catch the quick look that passed between her grandmother and Colonel Saunders.

"I'm sure he could, too," replied the Colonel gently, a faint smile playing about his lips.

"Well, I know you are in a hurry, Colonel, so if my other guests will excuse me for a few minutes I will show you those prints of mine," put in Lady Peebles as she rose to her feet. "Perhaps you would like to show Mr. and Mrs. Barking the garden, Vanessa—it is beginning to look quite springlike. And Jennifer, dear, I would be very grateful if you took Wendy out for me." Wendy was a small white sealyham that was the apple of her grandmother's eye.

Jennifer held open the door for the guests and then, remembering that she had left her rather grubby handkerchief behind, went back to retrieve it. She brushed past the small side-table that stood by her grandmother's chair and knocked a book on to the floor. As she bent down to pick it up she saw the letter lying open on the table. It was headed "The British Show Jumping Association".

Now Jennifer had been taught that it was a terrible thing to open other people's letters, but this one was open, and so, although she knew it was just as terrible to read it, she simply could not resist the temptation.

"Dear Lady Peebles. This is to confirm the registration of the 14–1 bay gelding Skipper that you purchased from Mr. Sam Dowling. He is Grade J.A. and now registered as such in your name, should you wish to jump him this season."

CHAPTER SEVEN

WHEN Jennifer returned home that evening she felt she was floating on a little pink cloud. Her Skipper was a Grade A pony already, and as Major Brentwood said, once Grade A always Grade A. Now she would not have to qualify for the White City; she could go there any time—this year, if she was allowed to. If only she could persuade her mother and father, if only she could! Granny, who had known all along about Skipper, had registered him. Surely that meant she was going to be allowed to jump him!

The telephone was ringing as they entered the house.

"I'd better take it, darling. I'm expecting a call," said Mrs. Charrington as Jennifer advanced to lift the receiver.

"Hullo, yes, this is 2115. Oh, hullo, Edith, I didn't recognise your voice. What? Oh no! My dear, I am most dreadfully sorry."

Jennifer stood stock still; the expression on her mother's face was enough without the words.

"Yes, yes—but of course, my dear. No, don't bother Norman. I'll go straight over there now. Mm—— Right, I'll do that. Goodbye."

"Mummy, Mummy, whatever is it? What's happened?"

"June has had an accident."

"An accident? Oh no, Mummy! Is she hurt? What happened?"

"Apparently the pony came down with her in the ring; hit the top of the wall very hard. They've taken her off to hospital in the ambulance."

"Is she badly hurt?"

"They're not sure. She has a broken arm, they think, but she is also unconscious."

Jennifer, who was doing a course of first-aid at school, was suddenly overcome by a terrifying thought. "Mummy, is it a fractured skull?"

Mrs. Charrington looked gravely at her daughter. "They are not sure; that is why I'm having Marigold here for the night, so Edith can stay at the hospital."

Major Brentwood met them on the doorstep, for he and Marigold had boxed the ponies home while Mrs. Brentwood went in the ambulance with June. "Edith rang to tell me that you were very kindly going to have Marigold. She's all ready."

"Any news?" queried Mrs. Charrington.

"She has recovered consciousness and they are X-raying her now. I'm just going over to the hospital myself. I'll call you when the result is through."

Marigold, looking very red about the eyes, sat silently in the car; no one spoke very much, and when they did it was about generalities like the weather. Mr. Charrington was waiting for them when they returned, armed with bottles of ginger pop. He talked long and heartily, going through his repertoire of funny stories to try and amuse the children.

"Come on, let's cook supper and give Mummy a surprise, shall we? Mrs. Long is out tonight." Anything, he thought, to keep the children occupied. "Omelette— a nice Spanish omelette," continued Mr. Charrington as they set to work.

He made Marigold peel the onions, for that would help to hide any real tears, while Jennifer beat the eggs. No one would feel like eating, but food was most important in a crisis. "I'll make the toast," he continued. "Omelettes and lashings of crisp hot toast. Don't you think that sounds super?"

His helpers nodded dumbly.

The kitchen, so spotless and tidy when they entered, soon looked as if a regiment of soldiers had passed hurriedly through, snatching something to eat as they went. Every plate, saucepan and bowl seemed to be in use; there was not a square inch on the kitchen table to put down even a knife. Mrs. Charrington took one agonised look from the door and withdrew hurriedly.

She had just walked across to the dining-room cupboard to pour herself out a sherry when the phone rang for the second time. She ran to the instrument. "Yes? Oh, Norman, I'm so glad. How wonderful! Yes, yes, I'll tell them."

The cooks had heard the bell too, and, regardless of burnt toast and congealed omelette, were waiting eagerly at her side.

"It's good news, thank heaven. June has slight concussion and her arm is a simple fracture."

"You mean," said Marigold, dropping the plate she was clasping with a clatter to the floor, "she is going to be all right?"

"Yes," said Mrs. Charrington brightly. "Quite all right. She'll have to stay in bed for a few days and she may have some bad headaches for a while, but——"

"And her arm?"

"Well, that will be in plaster, of course," put in Jennifer knowledgeably, "but it will probably come out straighter than it went in."

A thin cloud of pale blue smoke came wafting through the kitchen door.

"The toast, the toast," shouted Mr. Charrington.

"And my omelette," shrieked Jennifer.

The cooks flew back to the kitchen to rescue the supper, or what was left of it!

The room was filled with smoke and the acrid smell of burnt bread and eggs. This, coupled with the mess, resulted in Mrs. Charrington donning her apron and finishing the meal. They turned up the wireless and began to sing. The feeling of relief was so great that burnt food and an untidy kitchen seemed not to matter at all.

Jennifer decided that it was no good broaching the subject of jumping for the next few days. That would not be at all tactful. She would have to go quietly on with her riding and wait until June returned home before she mentioned anything about her plans. Now that Skipper was Grade A there was no immediate hurry.

June made a quick recovery and was allowed home much sooner than anyone expected. She still had to rest and take things quietly, but as she was allowed visitors Jennifer was naturally one of the first. In fact, she was there to greet her with fruit and flowers when she returned from the hospital.

During tea the afternoon post arrived and Marigold, who had answered the door, put a large buff-coloured envelope down beside her father.

"What's that, Daddy? It looks like a show schedule."

"It is: it's the International."

Jennifer jumped and dropped her spoon with a clatter in the saucer.

"We won't be able to go now, will we, Daddy?" queried Marigold.

"No, June will not be fit enough to get the pony qualified this year, and it's not worth taking the grey all the way up there on her own. Still, never mind, she'll be well enough to compete in most of the shows round here, and there's always next year."

Mrs. Charrington, who during this conversation had been toying with a cucumber sandwich, looked up quickly. "You mean, you're going to let her jump again, Norman?"

The Major looked faintly surprised. "Why, of course," he laughed. "We don't let falls like that worry us, do we, June?"

"Gracious, no," replied his daughter stoutly.

"Just a bit of bad luck that, but I bet the pony won't hit a wall again in a hurry."

Mrs. Charrington was quite nonplussed. To let the child ride again after a fall like that! It was incredible! She was about to say so too, in no uncertain fashion, when the complete matter-of-fact atmosphere and unconcerned expression on Edith Brentwood's face made her change her mind. Only seven days ago they had all been desperately worried waiting for the X-ray result, and now here they were calmly drinking tea and proposing to expose their child to the same danger in a few weeks' time. They must be mad!

Jennifer, taking her mother's silence for acceptance of the fact that falls make no difference, felt quite light-hearted and decided that the time had arrived when she could safely bring up the subject of herself and Skipper.

The journey home in the car proved as good a time as any. "You know, Mummy," she began tentatively, "after seeing Skipper jump that day in the field, you said you'd speak to Daddy. Have you?"

"No," replied Mrs. Charrington as she swung out to pass a Baby Austin car, "and I'm not going to."

"Not going to! But, Mummy, why?"

"Why? Well, I should have thought it was perfectly obvious after what's happened."

"B-but," spluttered Jennifer, "June's all right now, and they're going to let her jump again—and on that pony too. After all, Skipper is miles better; he wouldn't have done that."

"Don't talk nonsense, Jennifer. Any horse, however good, can make a mistake."

"Skipper wouldn't," she replied belligerently. "And you can't just stop doing things because a friend has had an accident—it—it's just stupid."

"Stupid or not," said her mother firmly, "you are not jumping Skipper in any show-ring."

"Supposing everyone said that," shouted Jennifer, getting redder and redder in the face. "Then no one would fly at all, or go on trains or drive a car. You didn't stop driving after you heard about Mrs. Dent's smash; Daddy didn't give up after the Arrowhead crash-landed that time and forbid the test pilot to fly again; Mrs.——"

"It's not a bit of good shouting, Jennifer. I've said No."

"I'll ask Granny, then she'll help me, she's bound to after buying me a pony like that."

"Like what?"

"Like Skipper. He's a Grade A show-jumping pony."

Mrs. Charrington gripped the steering-wheel firmly. "How do you know?" she whispered.

"Because I saw the letter from the B.S.J.A. saying so."

"Did Granny show it to you?"

"No, she left it lying on her table and I read it."

"Jennifer!"

"Oh, I know it was wrong, but I couldn't resist it. Skipper is good, Mummy, really good. He can jump at the International Horse Show."

"Well, he's not going to and neither are you, so let's change the subject, shall we?"

As they turned in through the gates of the Grange Jennifer started beating her fists on the dashboard. "Oh, it's not fair, it's not fair! June hasn't got nearly such a good pony and she had a bad fall, but she's allowed to carry on. I've got a super pony and ——"

"Jennifer, will you stop making that noise!"

"No, I won't, I won't," screamed the child. "It's so unfair. Everytime I want to do anything it's no, no, NO! Why do you let me walk—I might slip up and break my leg!"

"*Jennifer!*"

"No, I won't stop it!" screamed Jennifer, getting out of the car. "I hate being wrapped up in cotton wool, I hate it, I hate it. I *hate* it, I tell you. I hate everything." She jumped out, banged the car door behind her, and rushed into the house like a tornado.

"Good gracious," said Mr. Charrington, appearing on the door-step. "Whatever is the matter?"

"Jennifer is being quite impossible."

"So I heard. But what is it all about?"

"Because I said I wouldn't let her jump Skipper in any shows."

Mr. Charrington looked mystified. "But there wasn't any question of that, was there?"

His wife shook her head. "Not really—but I did say that I'd speak to you about it. That was before June's accident, though."

"Well, surely, after that——"

"You'd have thought so, wouldn't you? But the Brentwoods' allowing June to carry on doesn't help matters. Did you know that Skipper was a really first-class pony?"

"Only by what Jenkins has said. Actually I did approach your mother about it."

"And what did she say?"

"Oh, something about knowing good horse-flesh when she saw it."

"That's true, and this time is no exception. Apparently Skipper is a Grade A jumping pony, whatever that means."

"Top class, I think," replied her husband. "Your mother!"

"Don't say it, darling. I know; you wait till I see her! Oh, listen to that child! Please go up and speak to her, Gordon. She might as well hear it from you at the same time. Among other things, we do not want a tough, hardbitten, show-jumping fiend for a daughter. In short, she is *not* going to jump Skipper."

"All right, I'll go up and speak to her, if you'll ring the Trehernes and tell them we shall be late."

Mr. Charrington found Jennifer lying on the bed in floods of tears. He tried to talk to her sensibly, but she put her hands over her ears and sobbed, "Oh, go away, go away."

"Well, Jennifer," said her father sternly as he rose to go. "I'm ashamed of you—a big girl of your age behaving like this. I've a good mind to stop you riding altogether." Jennifer let out an agonised wail. "Well, pull yourself together then. You are an extremely lucky child to have a pony at all." He got up and quietly closed the door behind him.

Jennifer sobbed for a few minutes, her handkerchief a wet sodden ball. It was too awful for words. There was no point in anything any more; nothing to work for, or to look forward to. She sat up, and with her head held dejectedly between her hands gazed out of the window. A robin hopped upon the sill and looked at her with bright beady eyes. He chirruped away quite fearlessly, his little head on one side. "What's the matter?" he

seemed to say. "Nothing is so bad as all that. Why don't you sing and spread your wings like me and fly away into the lovely fresh air?" He flapped his wings, and with a final chirrup rose up into the soft spring sky.

Jennifer clutched her handkerchief more tightly. She would fly away too, like the little robin—all the way to the White City.

Why not? Her grandmother had once said to her, if you want anything hard enough and go all out to get it, you will in the end. And there was a film she had seen last holidays called *Never Take No for an Answer*. She got up and walked across to the window. She would never take no for an answer again, either; she would go to the White City, even if she had to run away to get there.

CHAPTER EIGHT

ONCE Jennifer made up her mind she seldom changed it, and she had made up her mind about the International Horse Show. She was going to compete there, whatever happened; nothing was going to stand in the way of her great ambition. Once that fact was firmly established in her mind she set about making plans. The first thing was to get hold of a schedule and, knowing the Brentwoods possessed one, she decided to cycle over there the following Saturday morning. She arrived to find June curled up in the big armchair in the playroom, deep in a book.

She glanced up as Jennifer came into the room. "Oh, hullo! Look, just let me finish this, will you? I've only got a few more pages and it's terribly exciting. There are some magazines on the table and the latest copy of *Horse and Hound*." June returned to her book.

Jennifer made a face but sat down obediently; there was nothing else to do. She flicked over the first pages and there she found it, the booklet with the white badge on the cover. "The International Horse Show. July 20–25. White City Stadium, London!" She stroked the cover fondly. Even the words sent little shivers up and down her spine. Glancing at the index she turned quickly to the Jumping Section. "The Preliminary Qualifying Competition for the Juvenile Championship (under F.E.I. Rules—Table (Bareme) 'A')." Good gracious, what did that mean? She read on. "Entry fee 40s." Two pounds! That was quite a lot. But remembering the twenty pounds in her Post Office Savings Bank, she cheered up, for one of the biggest stumbling blocks—the financial side of her escapade—would present no difficulties.

She continued to read on: "For registered ponies in Grade 'J.A.' at closing date of entries, not exceeding 14-2 hands, the property of Members of the B.S.J.A., to be ridden by Juvenile Members of the B.S.J.A." So far, all was well.

"Finished," sighed June. "Gosh, it was a good story. Well, what shall we do now?"

Jennifer started and looked up. "I dunno. How's the arm, by the way?"

"Oh, fine. It tickles frightfully, that's all. I keep having to scratch it with this pencil."

"Well, don't drop it down there," laughed Jennifer. "Let's have a look; you've got a lot more signatures on the plaster."

"Yes, James brought some friends in last week-end and they all insisted on autographing it. As I can use my fingers jolly well now, what about getting out the puppets?"

"Right," replied Jennifer, who had decided long ago that she had better not breathe a word of her plan to anyone, not even June. A secret such as hers had to be closely guarded if it was to succeed.

"Is Marigold going to show the grey pony at any of the big shows this summer?"

"No, I don't think so. He's very young, and as I can't go Daddy has decided to confine our activities to the local shows this year."

"It is a shame, especially when you might have been able to compete at the White City."

"Oh, well, I don't mind particularly. Don't you think this one is sweet?" June held up a small fairy. "Marigold made it last Sunday—she's getting jolly good."

Jennifer did not pursue the conversation further. She had found out all she wanted to know, namely that the Brentwoods would not require the schedule or its attendant entry form this year. Her immediate problem was to get hold of it. Asking for it might arouse June's curiosity—the last thing she wanted to do.

It was not until after tea that the opportunity arose, when June said: "Jennifer, be a dear and clear those papers off the table, will you? I want to touch up this piece of scenery. I'm getting so good with my fingers now that I can even paint."

"Right," replied Jennifer. "By the way, have you finished with the *Horse and Hound*?"

"Yes, take it home if you want to."

Jennifer needed no second bidding, so when six o'clock arrived she slipped the paper, which so neatly concealed its secret, into her bicycle basket and bore it home in triumph.

That night in bed she read it carefully from cover to cover, making a list of all the things she would have to do. It was quite a formidable one, and for the first time she felt a little doubt in the back of her mind. Could she do it? She shook her red curls and stuck our her chin determinedly. She was going to do it.

London was seventy miles away, and as the qualifying competition was early Saturday morning she would have to be there the night before. That meant getting a box for Skipper and a room for herself. She turned to the exhibitors' notes, and discovered that she could reserve a box for twenty-four hours for thirty shillings. It also mentioned that bedding was provided free and that she could purchase hay and feeding stuffs at the White City. But how was she to get there? She couldn't ride seventy miles, nor could she hire a motor horse-box, for neither its arrival nor her departure in it would go unnoticed.

No, there was only one answer—the pony would have to go by rail; and as she daren't go from her local junction in case she was recognised, it meant hacking over to Brently, a distance of fifteen miles. So one of the first things to do was to write to the station-master, asking him to reserve a horse-box to the Kensington (Olympia) station on Friday, July 24th.

Now came the burning question—what was she to call herself? If she used her own name she was certain to be found out fairly quickly, and if she used a fictitious one her entry might not be legal. She bit the end of her pencil, a worried frown on her face. It was quite a problem. Suddenly she decided to speak to Evans; as he was used to showing the Jersey cattle at the big agriculture shows he might be able to help, and provided she was tactful she need not give anything away.

She glanced at her watch. It was after ten o'clock, and if her mother came upstairs and found the light on she would have something to say. Jennifer slipped the precious schedule under her pillow and was soon fast asleep. She was in the ring at the White City and there were millions of people all clapping. She cleared the first fence and the second and the third, but they seemed never-ending. Every time she thought she was over the last, another loomed up in front of her. Then

F

suddenly the scene changed—she was galloping faster and faster over grass-covered fields. She must get to June's, she must get there, she must. The crowd had gone and she was alone with only the trees and the gathering night for company. She must get there——

"Are you all right, darling?" She awoke with a start to find her mother bending over her.

She rubbed her eyes. "Wh-what is it?"

"Nothing, darling, but I thought I heard you call out. You must have had a nightmare."

What had she said? She slipped her hand under the pillow and felt a terrific surge of relief as her fingers came in contact with the crinkling paper. The schedule was safe. She smiled as her mother bent down to kiss her goodnight.

The next morning she wandered down to the farm and found Evans checking the morning milk records in the clean, cool, white-washed dairy.

"How are the cows behaving? Giving gallons of milk?"

"Yes, Miss Jennifer. Old Daisy is expecting her sixth calf today."

"That was one of the first cows we had, wasn't it?"

"It was, and a grand one she's been too—given over nine hundred gallons each year, with a four per cent butter-fat content."

Jennifer nodded. "Are you showing any this season?"

"Yes, I'd thought we'd enter two heifers for the County Show in June and also that young bull we've got. He's going to be a champion, you mark my words."

"Do *you* enter them yourself? I mean, fill in the forms and everything."

"I do."

"I suppose Daddy has to sign them, though, doesn't he? It must be quite a business getting hold of him sometimes."

Evans grinned. "Oh, we don't have to bother him with entry forms. I sign them as his agent. We just let him know what we're going in for, and, if he can't be there, what we've won!"

Jennifer smiled. "And last year that was quite a lot, I know. I hope you do as well again this year."

So an agent could sign the entry forms! She ran back to her room and thumbed eagerly through the schedule, finding a note about it in the general rules at the back of the booklet under the heading "Authorised Agents". "Any entry form, objection or other document required by the Rules to be signed by an Exhibitor, may be accepted if signed on behalf of the Exhibitor by the agent whom the committee are satisfied is duly authorised to do so."

She would have to risk the committee! At last she knew what to do—she would enter the pony under her grandmother's name, Katherine Peebles, and sign the form J. Charrington, Agent—Rider, K. Charrington. That would be in order, as her second name was Katherine. If luck was with her she might get away with it.

She noted that the money had to be sent with the entry form, a total of three pounds ten shillings altogether, and as she did not possess a cheque book, postal orders for that amount would have to do. If anyone was grand enough to have an agent, they would naturally have a cheque book, but perhaps with the rush of entries they would overlook that point. It was a risk she had to take anyway.

"Jennifer, Jennifer!"

"Yes, Mummy?"

"I'm just going into Thaxted. Would you like to come?"

"Yes, please." It would give her the opportunity to get the postal orders in a general post office instead of under the piercing eye of Mrs. Couchman, the local village postmistress. "I won't be a second, I've only got to get my coat."

The first port of call was the chemist, at the opposite end of the town from the post office; so while her mother, armed with shopping basket and long list, disappeared in through the glass-fronted door, Jennifer remained in the car and turned on the wireless. The nostalgic strains of "Long Ago and Far Away" came pulsating over the ether, and as she hummed softly to herself her eyes came to rest on a large advertisement for hair dye in the adjoining shop. Skipper, with his two white stockings and white star, might be recognised; but if these were dyed? Jennifer leapt out of the car.

A peroxide blonde, filing her long red nails behind the counter in the hairdresser's, looked up with a sickly smile as Jennifer entered. "Yes?"

"I want two bottles of hair dye, please."

The blonde looked startled. "What colour, please?" She peered shortsightedly at Jennifer's fiery red curls.

"Dark brown." Then, noticing the girl's expression, she added hastily, "Oh, it's all right, it's not for me. It's for a friend."

After what seemed an interminable length of time, while endless drawers were opened and shut and a sample bottle of liquid shampoo was sent crashing to the ground, the dye was finally placed upon the counter with an old hair-net adhering to the bottom of one of the bottles. The girl pulled it off and threw it unceremoniously on to the floor, where it joined the shampoo.

"That will be seven shillings and sixpence, please."

Jennifer literally banged the money on the counter, stuffed the bottles in her pocket and fled, hoping against hope that her mother would not be in the car waiting for her. All was well—the little Morris was empty except for the beat of drums and the crash of cymbals. There was nothing if not variety in the "Music while you Work" programme.

Jennifer returned to the Grange just before lunch feeling very jubilant; for not only had she acquired the postal orders, the stamps and the hair dye, but the name of a suitable hotel in London where she could stay.

Running into Mrs. Lambert, a large flamboyant woman, in the greengrocer's, they had been treated to a detailed account of her recent trip to the big city, to the intense amusement of the other customers. Her voice was loud and strident.

"And, my dear, I found the most marvellous hotel in Kensington. It's just opened, so comfortable and so reasonable"—she lowered her voice and mumbled into Mrs. Charrington's ear—"and that with a private bath as well. My dear, you simply must try it."

"I will," replied Mrs. Charrington, "but you haven't told me the name of it yet."

"Oh, how stupid of me, my dear. The Camberley in Harwell Gardens. Yes, yes, I said three lemons!" The poor assistant, looking slightly harassed, was trying to cope with her order. As she changed it every minute and was giving it between sentences of her story, it was proving a well-night impossible task.

Jennifer grinned as she recalled the scene and then, glancing down again at the hair dye, began to think of the job in hand. Skipper was going to be all right, he would be disguised; but what about herself? After all, red curls were rather distinctive. She debated whether she would dye them too, but fingering one of the curls lovingly she decided against that idea; it was not only drastic but of a much too permanent nature.

Suddenly she remembered the dressing-up clothes in the attic. Mrs. Charrington had at one time been very interested in amateur dramatics, and sometimes still produced a play in the village. This, coupled with a variety of fancy-dress costumes, left-overs from her youthful days at Eastly Manor, resulted in a large selection of costumes.

Jennifer, torch in hand, climbed the stairs to the dim dark roof and began to rummage amongst the trunks and old tin boxes. Everything seemed to have found its

way up to there—all the things that might come in useful
one day lay discarded and entirely forgotten amongst
the dust and the cobwebs. The thin beam of the torch
travelled like a long enquiring finger around the eaves
and came to rest at last on some cardboard boxes.
Jennifer, treading gingerly over old pictures and photo
frames, bent down to read the writing on the lid. Pierrot
Costume, it said, and on the next was Flower Seller,
until finally, at the bottom of the pile, she came across
one marked Elizabethan Page-boy. She lifted the lid
and there, on top of the midnight-blue jacket, lay a
black wig with a fringe. Slipping it underneath her
jacket in case she should meet anyone, Jennifer returned
to her room.

The wig fitted her beautifully, but as it looked a
trifle old-fashioned she took up the scissors and cut off
about an inch all round.

"Ah, that's better," muttered Jennifer, as she looked
at herself in the glass. "But if I move my head quickly
those bottom curls do show a wee bit. Still, it's the
White City or curls, and I've chosen the White City."

She surveyed herself again. There was something
wrong. Of course! No one had jet-black hair and red-
gold eyebrows and lashes. She would have to pay a visit to
the cosmetic counter at Netherburys when next she
went to Thaxted and rectify that.

Hearing footsteps on the landing, she thrust the wig
hastily under the eiderdown, swept the purchases of the
morning hurriedly into a drawer and sat down to brush
her hair.

Mrs. Long, the daily, put her head round the door.
"Ah, there you are. Didn't you hear your mother
calling? She wants you downstairs."

CHAPTER NINE

JENNIFER, knowing that the London mail usually arrived by the first post in the morning, got up early each day to intercept the postman, for she dare not have the answers to her letters arriving at the house.

The first reply was from the hotel confirming a single room for the night of July 24th. She felt very grown up receiving a letter from a London hotel that began " Dear Madam ".

The next day there was one from the station-master at Brently to say that he had reserved a box which would be coupled to the 12.45 p.m. to London, enabling her to make the necessary connection to the Kensington (Olympia) station, arriving there at 5.45 p.m. The cost of the box would be two pounds sixteen shillings and fourpence; and as that left thirteen pounds, eleven shillings and eightpence after all initial expenses had been paid, it would be more than enough to cover everything else.

Three days passed and there was still no reply from the International. Could they be making enquiries as to whether she was really an agent? Perhaps the postal orders had aroused their suspicions? Jennifer began to feel very worried.

Driving home from school one afternoon, her mother spotted the postman and slowed down. "Ask him if there are any letters for us, darling, will you? It will save him coming down the drive."

Jennifer rolled down the window of the car. "Anything for us, please, Tedder?"

The man got off his bicycle. "Yes, I think there is." He took out a pile of letters tied up with string. "Ah, here we are. There are two, and one of them for you." He smiled.

Jennifer froze with horror, for the white envelope had the words "International Horse Show" on it.

She took the letters with a trembling hand and quickly turned the telltale envelope face downwards so her mother would not see it.

"Anything interesting?"

"Yours is from America, it looks like Aunt Dolly's writing."

"Oh, good. I was waiting to hear from her. What's yours? It looks very impressive."

Jennifer clutched it tightly. "Stop, Mummy! Look— one of the calves has got through into the garden." She could have hugged the little animal for providing such a welcome diversion. With any luck now, her mother would forget to enquire further and she had not had to tell a deliberate lie. The thought of lying to her parents made her feel sick inside. If she did not have to actually say anything untrue she would not feel so bad about the great adventure.

As soon as the calf had been chased from the smooth green lawn to its proper abode in the adjoining field Jennifer made a wild dash for the house and the seclusion of her room.

Slitting open the envelope, she felt almost afraid to withdraw the contents in case anything had gone wrong. All was in order—her box was reserved for the night and her entry had been accepted. She leaned back in

her chair and surveyed the papers with triumph. She was a competitor in the International Horse Show! She felt herself grow in stature at the mere thought of it.

After most of the business side of the venture had been arranged Jennifer set to work in earnest, both with her riding and the task of getting Skipper really fit. As he had to remain out it presented quite a problem, for she could hardly suggest, after a long winter, that the pony be kept in now during the summer months, when the weather was warm and the grass sweet. She knew, though, that she would have to feed him well. He must have at least six pounds of oats a day. Luckily she had kept up his small feeds, as he was in regular work; but it was going to be a little tricky stepping up the oats without a few questions being asked, especially as all the feeding stuffs were checked, and so Evans knew almost to the pound what was being used. If she made a point of riding every evening she could say that Skipper seemed sluggish and ought to have more food, as he was working so hard. In this way she might get his allowance stepped up to four pounds a day, and perhaps, with any luck, no one would notice the other two pounds for a little while. She rode him regularly and did a lot of schooling, getting him to answer to the slightest touch of the hand and leg. She jumped him, too, round the small fences in the field at least twice a week under the capable eye of Jenkins.

One evening she decided to approach him. "Jenkins, couldn't we make the fences more interesting? Both Skipper and I know them backwards."

The man scratched his head thoughtfully. "Well," he muttered, "I don't know as I've time to make any more."

"Oh, it doesn't matter about new ones. I could paint the existing ones different colours and then we could put them at all sorts of angles."

"Like them courses they have in the shows nowadays, you mean?"

Jennifer nodded.

"All right, we can do that. Might be a good idea and all—get you to really control that pony. I think you're progressing well enough; and, what's more, I'll get you jumping a single straight pole too."

Jennifer had great fun with a large brush and the remains of various cans of paint that had been used about the farm. She made the jumps as brilliant and outrageous as possible.

Her mother, finding her squatting on the lawn, her dungarees spattered with vermilion, green and white, was slightly annoyed.

"It's O.K., Mummy, don't worry; they're my very old pair, the ones that are nearly through at the seat."

"But what are you doing?"

"Painting the fences Jenkins made for me, to make them look smart."

"What an extraordinary idea, and what a waste of time!" Mrs. Charrington paused at a particularly jazzy example. "Skipper won't shy at these and bolt, will he?"

Jennifer laughed. "Of course not. They won't be any higher, and they'll knock down just as easily; so don't worry, Mummy."

"Well, if Jenkins knows all about it, I suppose it's all right," she said dubiously. "I'll go and have a word with him now."

The man must have reassured her, for they proceeded with their programme. As the days progressed she got more and more confident, and felt really one with her pony, jumping small doubles and trebles and poles at different distances apart, sometimes approaching the next fence on a diagonal.

The more Jenkins saw of them the more convinced he became that the pair would go right to the top if they were only allowed to try. It did seem a pity, especially with a child as keen as Jennifer.

The time passed fairly quickly. June gave way to July and the Show was drawing very near. She wished that she could jump once round the big schooling field at the Brentwoods' before she finally set out, but it seemed quite impossible, for she had promised not to jump over there in their presence. So it was with a feeling of intense delight that she learned the whole family was going off for the weekend.

The jumping field was away from the farm buildings, so if she rode over there on the Saturday and picked a good time—early afternoon before milking—she might get away with it. It was worth trying.

Setting out after lunch, ostensibly for a gentle ride, she took the short cut and came out at the bottom of the Brentwoods' land. Everything was peaceful, wrapped in the gentle afternoon haze. The cows, half asleep, were peacefully chewing the cud and flicking off the flies with their long tails. A dragonfly rose from some nearby foliage and hovered over the small stream, its wings a transparent rainbow glinting in the sun. Summer—that magic season, when the world is heady with maturity, when it has reached the peak of its fulfilment. Jennifer yawned and brushed a fly off her nose. She rode along the high hedgerows to the jumping field. No one was in sight and what was even more fortunate, the fences were up at the regulation height, so she would not have to waste precious minutes getting them ready. The jumps had been altered slightly, so she would pretend this was the real thing and walk the course first. She slipped a halter over Skipper's bridle and hitched him to a post. There was a triple combination fence and a small water, which was something quite new.

She went back and cantered Skipper round once or twice before going over to the practice fence. Glancing at her watch she saw that it was three o'clock. She would have to hurry to get away before the men returned for feeding and milking.

Skipper, his ears pricked as he cantered into the first fence, went well, and Jennifer, who felt a different person after the last few weeks, was much more confident. They jumped quite a successful round, making only one mistake at the stile.

She slipped to the ground and gave him a knob of sugar. "Good boy, good boy," she whispered.

There was a distant sound of voices, so mounting hurriedly, she rode off down the field and had just reached the gate at the far end when the head cowman popped his head over it. "Hullo. Looking for Miss June? They've all gone away for the weekend."

Jennifer smiled. "I know, but I forgot all about it until I got here, which was stupid of me. Still, as it's a lovely day, it doesn't matter."

"Yes, it's proper summery like, now. 'Ope it keeps up like this till after the 'arvest."

As they walked home Jennifer turned over the problems in her mind. Owing to her disguise, she knew she would have to make a really early start and leave the Grange before five fifteen, a good three-quarters of an hour before the men arrived to milk. As Skipper was in the small paddock away from the cows the men would be unlikely to notice his disappearance at such an early hour. One good thing too was that the school holidays would have begun, and as she often went for an early morning ride no one would miss her until breakfast. If she could convey the impression that she was going over to the Brentwoods' without actually saying so it might help to extend the time before the alarm was given.

It was getting near now. She felt very excited and not a little nervous, for it was really a terrific adventure. She patted Skipper's neck. "You've no idea where we are going to be in a fortnight's time," she whispered.

CHAPTER TEN

B R-R-R went the alarm clock. Jennifer dived
beneath the bed-clothes, frantically trying to stop
it, for surely the whole house must have heard
the din—it sounded like a dozen fire alarms. When
she had tried it the previous day only the faintest tinkle
had emanated from the bottom of the bed. She lay
waiting, listening and trembling from head to foot. But
no one stirred; the house, clothed in its mantle of sleep,
was as still as death, so getting silently out of bed, she
started to dress.

As she had packed her rucksack the night before, only
the actual disguise was left to be done. First of all came
the heart-breaking business of cutting off the lower
curls, but with each snip of the scissors she felt one step
nearer her goal. This accomplished, she fitted on the
wig, pinning it firmly to the rest of her hair, for it would
be terrible if it blew off in a gust of wind, and con-
templating this disaster, she pushed a further two
packets of hair pins into her pocket. Next came the
eyebrows, which she traced out carefully with the
sharp black eyebrow pencil, then the eyelashes. Ugh!
What horrible stuff mascara was! She stuck the brush
in her eye and wept copious tears, making the eyeblack
run. At last it was done, and Jennifer stood back to
survey the finished effect in the looking-glass. Goodness!
She was completely different! She pinched herself to
make certain that it was really Jennifer Charrington and

not some impostor. "Well," she sighed happily, "if I don't recognise myself, no one else will." And with that she stuffed her eye make-up things into the rucksack and, shoes and one bottle of dye in hand, started to creep down the stairs.

Creak! She had forgotten the loose board on the landing just outside her parents' room. Holding her breath, she pressed hard against the wall, hoping to become one with the shadows. A long-drawn-out snore hovered on the still night air; her father was lying on his back again. On she crept, down the oak staircase, trying to remember which particular stairs creaked more than others. And so she came to the kitchen, feeling more as if she had crossed a treacherous mountain crevice than merely negotiated the familiar journey down her own front staircase. The curtains were drawn still, so the darkness and the stillness magnified everything a hundredfold.

She ate her breakfast—a glass of milk and a hunk of bread and butter—much as the Jews must have devoured the Feast of the Passover, before making the final check of her belongings. The railway ticket, the reserved box at the White City, money, toothbrush, saddle-soap and sponge, small tin of Brasso, shoe polish, clothes brush, clean gloves, and finally a lipstick. She had decided at the last minute to pretend to be a grown-up, a girl groom up for the International Horse Show, when she went to the hotel, for they might be suspicious of a child staying there alone. All was in order, so she crept out of the back door and round to the small paddock where she left the rucksack. Then, keeping to the grass verge, she made her way round to the yard to collect the saddle and bridle and Skipper's midday feed. The forage room was dark, and as the pale beam of her torch cast a wavering pathway between the bins Jennifer saw, caught like a plane in a searchlight beam, a large black rat. She stifled a scream and stood rooted to the spot while the rat, mesmerized by the light, stared back. Jennifer's hand shook, the light flickered and the rat scuttled away into the shadows. Jennifer stamped her feet and coughed to warn any other rats of her presence before she measured out the feed; then, making her way to the tack-room, picked up the bridle, saddle and halter.

Skipper came across the field at the sound of her voice. He was very easy to catch, for he was keen on his tummy, and as Jennifer spelt food to him he needed no second bidding.

Slipping the halter on, she led him into the shed and set about dyeing his two white socks. The star she decided to leave, in case, if he tossed his head, any of the dye got into his eyes. Skipper sniffed the air and then looked round at her with interest. What on earth was going on?

At exactly a quarter to five she mounted Skipper and rode out across the dew-soaked grass. The journey had begun.

As they came to the little pillar-box by the side of the grey stone bridge Jennifer leaned over and slipped an envelope through its ever-open mouth. It was addressed to her parents and said: "Darling Mummy and Daddy, Please do not worry, I am quite safe. See you Sunday. Much love, Jennifer."

It would be delivered at about four in the afternoon and as it was Welfare Day her mother would not be home until then. She had managed to convey, also, that she was going to the Brentwoods, so no one else would be

G

unduly disturbed by her absence. Once the letter was on its way she felt better and not nearly so guilty about the whole affair. There would be no need for them to worry any more, for they would know that she was well and safe and had not been killed or kidnapped. This thought made her feel much happier, and she began to hum the old tune "Keep right on to the End of the Road, Keep right on to the End".

"We'll do that all right, won't we, Skipper?" she whispered as she patted his neck.

The eastern sky was a pearly pink, the air fresh and clean, and a lark, high on the wing, sent its sweet notes up to heaven like a prelude to beauty, a herald's song to the morn. The veils of night had vanished, the earth was astir, alive, pulsating and vibrant. Only the human animals were asleep, missing the best of the day, and to Jennifer, who had never been abroad quite so early before, it was a new experience and one that would live long in her memory.

They passed a farm labourer on his way to work. "Good morning, Miss, you be up early."

Jennifer smiled. "This is the nicest time of the day."

"Must be hiking or something with that pack on her back—queer idea and by 'erself too; but then, youngsters be independent and queer in these toimes. Now in my young days," and he wandered on, muttering idly to himself.

They came at last to a small, moss-covered dell with a stream rippling through it, and as Skipper lowered his head to drink Jennifer decided that this was the ideal place for a rest. The time was eight o'clock, and as they had covered ten miles only five separated them now from Brently. She hitched Skipper to a tree with the halter, took the heavy rucksack from her shoulder with a sigh of relief and sat down on the moss. She yawned. It was beautifully peaceful.

Exactly how long she slept she was never quite sure, but when her eyes once more opened upon the same scene the pony had vanished. She leapt to her feet feeling sick with horror and apprehension.

"Skipper, Skipper," she called in anguish as she stumbled through the wood. But only the echo of her own voice answered her.

Oh, why had she fallen asleep? How could she have been so unutterably stupid? Were all her plans and dreams and hopes to end like this? "Skipper, Skipper." She sat down on a tree trunk and burst into tears.

"This your pony, Miss?"

Jennifer looked up to see a red-faced man holding a rather dejected-looking pony.

"Y-yes." She dabbed her eyes. "Where did you find him?"

"In the cornfield yonder 'elping 'isself."

"Oh, I'm so sorry. I hope he didn't do any damage."

"No, 'e didn't get time for that."

She pulled out her purse and gave the man the half a crown. "Thank you so very much for catching him."

The man grinned and touched his cap. "Thank'ee, Miss. Are you all right?"

"Yes, thank you," said Jennifer with a puzzled frown.

"You ain't 'urt your eye, 'ave you?"

She put her hand up and found it black with mascara. "The pony broke loose while I was asleep; I must have laid my head on some mud or something."

The man nodded. "So long as you're all right, Miss."

"Yes, I'm fine now I've got the pony."

Jennifer mounted, rode back to the dell, repaired her eye make-up, collected her rucksack and resumed the journey.

The station at Brently was on the outskirts of the old market town, and as she rode up the tarmac incline the clock pointed to twelve noon. She was in good time, three-quarters of an hour before the train was due to start. Finding the station-master, she learned that all was in order and the box waiting in the siding.

"I'll get a porter to give you a 'and, Miss. I 'ope you 'as luck at the Show."

"Thank you," replied Jennifer.

As she looked around at the deserted platform she felt an icy finger touch her heart, for there is nothing so desolate as an empty station. It seemed as if all the comings and goings, the heartbreak and the laughter of this centre of travel and ceased for ever. The wind caught an old piece of newspaper and whirled it round and round the grey platform until it fell, as if exhausted, upon the wooden sleepers beneath. A faint smell of fish permeated the air; nothing stirred; it might be the last station on the line, the station of the dead. Then a signal clicked, a uniformed man appeared clasping two flags, some porters popped like rabbits from a hole and began to look busy, there was the distant rumble of wheels, metal on metal, the station became alive—a train was coming.

Jennifer turned Skipper to face it, for a horse is never so afraid of what it can see. He flicked his ears, shivered and backed away as the engine thundered past, but that was all.

After the local train had puffed busily on its way two porters came up arguing fiercely about the day's racing.

"This the pony?" asked the first one, pointing a greasy finger at Skipper.

"No, Alf, that ain't it. It's sitting in the waiting-room, waiting for you to go and tell it the time of the train," replied Alf's mate sarcastically.

"Oh, dry up," growled the other, who disliked being made fun of. "Ain't you going to put no bandages or nothing on 'is legs?"

"Oh," said Jennifer. "I've forgotten them!"

"Just loike a girl," muttered Alf. "I'll see if I can find any. You see, we 'as more 'orses to deal with at this 'ere station than 'umans sometimes, so we keeps a few things in stock, like."

A few minutes later Alf appeared carrying a set of dirty, moth-eaten bandages, which Jennifer put on while the porter stood at the pony's head.

"All set now? We'll put 'im in, shall we?"

Jennifer nodded. "I'll lead him."

Skipper, who was used to travelling, walked quietly up behind her and into the box. She tied him up and slipped the feed into the manger before the men put up the partition.

"O.K. now?"

"Yes. Thank you very much for helping me," she added as she gave them a small tip each.

They were shunted round, and at twelve forty-five to the minute were coupled on to the London train. The second part of the journey had begun.

CHAPTER ELEVEN

T HE train with one tremendous shudder began
to move slowly out of the station, the engine
puffing and panting like a person who is short of
breath. Jennifer slid back the panel and peeped at
Skipper. He seemed quite unconcerned and was
devouring his food with obvious relish.

She decided to follow his example and opened the
packet of ham sandwiches which Alf the porter had
procured from the station canteen. They were fresh,
and instead of one minute slice of ham nestling self-
consciously between two doorsteps of bread there
was quite a respectable chunk of it.

Jennifer munched away contentedly and watched the
landscape slide past like a motion picture. The cattle
clustered round a pond, their tails moving incessantly,
whisking the flies off themselves and their compatriots,
their feet in the cool water; then the fields of grain, the
deep gold of the wheat and the silver gold of the barley,
waving in the breeze like sunlight on the sea; the mellow
rose of old tiles on a barn; the bright chequer-board of
fields melting away to the horizon. England lay before
her, small and neat, yet perfect in its placid, ordered
beauty. There was too much to see from the window of
a train to bury one's head in a book.

Jennifer began to play the hunting game. Hounds
were running and they were galloping across the narrow
field in the valley, out of that and over a post and rails

into a field of plough (it was barley now, but in winter it
would be plough). They galloped along beside the
hedge and over the thorn fence with the big ditch on the
landing side and into pasture again. Oh dear, how could
she get out of that? The train gathered speed. It would
mean jumping into a lane and it looked as if there was
wire too. The train, however, did not pause to let her
find out. That was the trouble with the hunting game,
one had to cheat sometimes to keep up.

The wheels beat a steady rhythm as they rolled along
the rails and Jennifer, lulled by the sound, dozed off into
dreamland to the accompaniment of their chatter. "You
will win; no, you won't; you will win; no, you won't."

She awoke to find the countryside studded with
bungalows, villas and large advertisements. London
was spreading its ugly tentacles further and further into
the country. The villas merged into factories and the
factories into rows of houses and shops. They were
nearing the heart of the greedy city.

After what seemed a lifetime of being shunted round
a maze of lines and yards and stations, they finally came
to rest at the Kensington station where, with the help
of some cockney porters, Skipper was unboxed.

Jennifer removed the bandages and handed them to
one of the porters. "Railway property, I think. I
borrowed them at the start of the journey."

The porter grinned. "Well, what do you know?
Going to the White City?"

"Yes," replied Jennifer. "Do you know it?"

"'Course I do—go there every Saturday."

"But it's only on for a week."

"What do you mean?" The man looked puzzled for
a second, then, flinging back his head, he roared with

laughter. "Cor luv a duck, they don't only have 'orse shows there, Miss. I go to the Dogs."

It was Jennifer's turn to look puzzled. "Go to the Dogs?" That meant he was very bad. Surely he didn't mean that? He had such an open friendly face.

"Yes, I takes the missus every Saturday."

This was worse than ever.

"She just likes to see the grey'ounds tearing round, but I likes my little bet. There's no betting at the 'orse show, they tell me—more's the pity. Now, if you could put a shilling or two on them jumpers, that would be sport."

Jennifer smiled with relief. He wasn't really so bad, after all. The porter went with her to the station entrance. "Not used to Lunnon, are you?"

"No-no," replied Jennifer uncertainly.

"Well, you take my advice—go up there on your feet, leading that there pony. The traffic's very 'eavy round 'ere at this hour. An' good luck to you; mind you win a prize."

Jennifer took the man's advice thankfully, for the hustle and bustle quite terrified her, and even Skipper, who usually never turned a hair in traffic, was jumpy. Taxis hooted, cars swished past and the buses chugged patiently along with their cargo of humanity. The road was hot underfoot, it seemed to burn into her shoe leather; the leaves on the few visible trees were dust laden and weary; and the air, heavy with petrol fumes, smoke and garbage, made Jennifer devoutly glad that she did not have to live in London. The tall grey houses wore their grime like uniform and it seemed to Jennifer that the constant outlook of smoke, bustle and buildings had seared into them, making them mean and soulless, so unlike the welcoming façade of the humblest country cottage.

They came to the lights at the end of Holland Road and turned left into the burly-hurly. Everybody seemed to be in a tearing hurry: they had to get to their destination the quickest and shortest way. No one ever explained what they did with the time they saved—that was the fallacy of the modern age.

Jennifer came to the Shepherds Bush roundabout and turned right. She gripped the reins more tightly as all the traffic seemed to bear down on her hooting and screaming. She stopped dead and shook. People shouted, but she had no idea what they were saying, and their wild gesticulations only confused her more. She felt sick with horror as a large red bus came straight towards her and swung out to pass at what seemed the last possible second.

"'Ere, Miss, you can't go up there, it's a one-way street." The policeman in his dark blue uniform and helmet assumed the role of a fairy godmother instead of the strong arm of the law. He put Jennifer on the right road and explained the mysteries of roundabouts and one-way traffic.

A yellow notice high on a lamp-post had the magic words "White City" painted on it, with an arrow pointing straight ahead. Another five minutes and the flags came into view, and then there were sounds other than the roar of traffic—the *clop, clop* of horses' feet. They had arrived!

After handing in her admission card at the road entrance, she noted the number of her box and then went along to report to the stable manager. It was a wonderful feeling to know that on every side were

horses: famous jumpers, hacks, hunters, and children's ponies. Here in the centre of the machine-minded city, like a great oasis in a vast desert, were gathered the first friends of man.

She was glad to find the box quite roomy, with a liberal supply of peat bedding, and after Jennifer had unsaddled and brushed the pony down, she went off in search of water and food. She bought hay, oats, bran and chaff and staggered back to the box, where she gave Skipper a good grooming while he munched his hay.

At half-past six she decided to go across in search of something to eat herself. She could not give the pony his last feed until seven-thirty at the earliest, and so, by the time she reached her hotel, dinner would most definitely be off. Besides, trying to be a grown-up was going to be a terrible strain and might arouse a lot of awkward questions, so the less time spent at the hotel the better.

She walked across the road and in through the big wooden doors. She was inside the White City at last! Even though the call of the stomach was strong, the call of the big arena was stronger, and she had to see what it looked like through her own eyes and not through those of the television camera—her only experience of the International up-to-date.

She clutched the white railings and drank in the sheer magic of it. The clean bright fences with their little tubbed trees on either side, the Union Jack fluttering from the centre flagpole which was banked high with flowers, the great clock that ticked off the precious seconds, the inner collecting ring, the giant tiered stands, the Royal Box, the members' enclosure, and round the outside and above, like sentinels, flew the flags of the competing nations. It lay before her in all its colour and glory, alive and real instead of on the black-and-white screen; and the atmosphere that permeated every corner of the place, the feeling of tensed excitement, friendly rivalry and international goodwill were more wonderful than she had ever dreamed.

The evening session began at seven o'clock, and as the first competition was an International Jumping Class Jennifer dashed off in search of a sandwich and a cup of tea and returned in time to see the competitors walking the course. They studied each fence carefully, and some paced out the distance between them. It was a great help to see at close quarters the fences one was called upon to negotiate. Punctually to the minute the first horse cantered into the arena, a compact little bay ridden by one of the Irish team. The officer pulled up in front of the Royal Box and saluted.

As Jennifer watched each competitor go round she realised that the twisty courses contributed quite a memory test as well as all the other hazards. Show-jumping as practised by these experts was a highly skilful game.

The competition—a Bareme C one—was judged on time, every fault counting so many seconds and added on to the time taken to complete the course. One girl, a brilliant rider, rode so smoothly that it was not until one looked at the clock that one realised she was knocking seconds off the previous record. Jennifer watched her taking the shortest route between fences so skilfully that the spectacular gallops of some of the competitors seemed like an amateur performance beside hers. She neared the last fence, and the crowd held their breath. Up and over, and the stillness was shattered with a burst of applause. Her time was one minute fifteen seconds, five seconds faster than the nearest rival. The rest had something to beat and the competition got very exciting —especially when an Irishman looked like lopping off a further two seconds. He approached the last fence a trifle too fast, the horse hesitated, got off its legs and hit the top bar. So the English girl, riding the grey, was acclaimed the winner. The Union Jack fluttered from the central flag-pole as the victors lined up in front of the Royal Box, and even the horses stood to attention as "God Save the Queen" was played. That was one of the exciting things about the International Horse Show, the ceremony and the wonderful pageantry.

Jennifer was very tempted to stay for the rest of the evening, but early bed was essential if she was going to be fit to ride the next day, so reluctantly she left the place of enchantment and went across to give Skipper his last feed. After telling the stable manager that she was off for the night, she collected her rucksack and made her way to the Underground station.

She took the tube to Kensington; and going into the cloakroom there, she dusted her face with powder and gingerly applied the lipstick. Her black hair, pale face and brilliant gash for a mouth made her look very grown-up. She squared her shoulders; she was alone in the big, bad city—a girl groom up for the Horse Show. She must act well and not forget her part.

The reception desk at the hotel was empty, and she felt rather self-conscious standing there all alone, while the occupants of the silver-grey lounge looked her up and down. One old lady, carefully lifting the pince-nez that hung round her neck on a black silken cord, peered intently at Jennifer, shaking her head the while. The child felt acutely embarrassed—was it so obvious that she was masquerading as an adult? Then suddenly the truth dawned on her—they were staring because of her clothes. Riding kit in London at nine in the evening.

After several minutes she pressed the bell on the desk and a bald-headed man with large horn-rimmed spectacles appeared from the office behind. Yes?"

"I booked a room for one night."

"The name, madam?"

"Miss Char—Miss Peebles, Miss Katherine Peebles."

"Oh, yes, Number 35. Have you any luggage, madam? I'll get the porter to take it up for you."

She swallowed hard at the 'madam.' "No; only a small overnight bag, thank you. I can manage that myself."

"Very good, madam. Number 35 is on the second floor. Do you require a call in the morning?"

"Oh yes, please," replied Jennifer.

"And tea at what time?"

Jennifer thought quickly. "As I have to be at the White City early, seven o'clock, please."

"Would you like your bill now, then, madam?"

"Yes, please."

"With early tea that will be thirty shillings."

Jennifer paid the bill, and as she bent down to pick up her rucksack the chime of Big Ben shattered the silence of the sedate lounge.

"This is the B.B.C. Home Service. Before the news here is a police message. Missing from home at Merton Boundary, Jennifer Charrington." She stopped dead, clutching the strap of the rucksack like a drowning man might clutch at a straw. "Aged 14 years, height 5 ft. 1 in., with red curls, pale complexion and blue eyes. Dressed in jodhpurs and tweed jacket and riding a bay pony with two white hind socks. Will anyone able to give any information please communicate with New Scotland Yard, telephone number Whitehall 1212."

CHAPTER TWELVE

EVEN though she was terribly tired, Jennifer kept waking up and peering at the luminous dial of her watch. She could not sleep properly, for she was far too nervous and strung up. It disturbed her, too, to think that her parents were in such a panic. She would have loved to get in touch with them and tell them once again not to worry, but to do that would only give away her whereabouts. Childlike, it rather surprised her to know that they were so unduly upset after the note she had sent them.

Finally, at six-thirty she clambered out of bed. She could not stay there for one second longer without knowing how Skipper had fared after his night in a strange stable. Her morning tea forgotten, she crept down the thickly carpeted stairs, across the empty lounge and so out into the street. London was astir, the late-night revellers had returned to bed, and the city now echoed with the feet of the early workers—the paper-delivery vans and the milk carts. The sun was up and the sky cloudless; another day had begun.

Skipper, his head over the box and his ears pricked, saw her coming down the line of boxes and nickered in greeting. He was fine. She refilled the bucket of water and gave him his first feed, then set about grooming and strapping him in preparation for the great event.

By eight o'clock her head was aching badly, and she felt empty and faintly sick. She straightened up and

peered over the stable door. The place was swarming
with people and grooms, and with so much activity
there must be surely a canteen open somewhere in the
vicinity. Breakfast might help the terrible sinking feeling
in her tummy. She went across to investigate, and a buzz
of voices and a rattle of tea-cups greeted her first timid
glance through the door.

Suddenly she felt very lost and lonely and afraid.
Everyone seemed to know everyone else, and the children had grown-ups to cheer and support them. She
stirred her tea and felt a lump rising in her throat. If
only there was one familiar face, one person to steady
her and tell her what to do and where to go.

"Have you seen a plan of the course yet?" said a voice
beside her.

Jennifer pricked up her ears.

"No, Penny, I haven't. I'm going along after I've
had something to eat. What's it like?" asked a tough,
fair-haired girl.

"Not too bad—there are eleven fences. The worst
part of the whole thing is I'm drawn number one. I
loathe having to go early in the competition. I'm sure
to forget the course or something."

There was a plan of the course, then, and a draw as to
the position in which you jumped! Jennifer decided to
follow behind the fair-haired girl and find out all she
could.

The plan was pinned to a big notice-board in the outer
collecting ring and beside it was the list of competitors,
together with their numbers and the order in which
they were to jump. She glanced hurriedly down the
names. Katherine Peebles, number three hundred and
ninety-three. Drawn twenty-four. That meant she

H

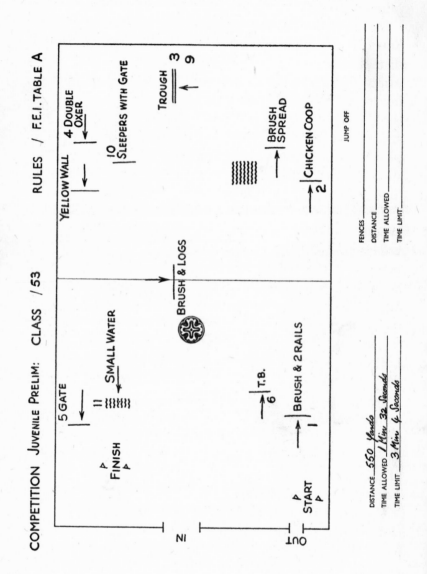

COMPETITION JUVENILE PRELIM: CLASS / 53 RULES / F.E.I. TABLE A

5 GATE
11
SMALL WATER
FINISH

T.B.
6
BRUSH & 2 RAILS
1

BRUSH & LOGS

YELLOW WALL 4 DOUBLE OXER
10 SLEEPERS WITH GATE
TROUGH 3
9

BRUSH SPREAD
CHICKEN COOP 2

START

IN
OUT

JUMP OFF

FENCES
DISTANCE
TIME ALLOWED
TIME LIMIT:

DISTANCE 550 Yards
TIME ALLOWED 1 Min 32 Seconds
TIME LIMIT 3 Min 6 Seconds

would have quite a long time to wait before she actually jumped.

At the bottom of the board there was a notice under-lined in red ink: "Competitors may view the course dismounted at 9.45 a.m." It said also: "Horses must jump in the order in which they appear on the notice-board, unless special permission has been obtained from the director of jumping events. This regulation will be strictly enforced." There was no chance of swapping places with anyone—very different from the smaller shows June talked about. Everything was most pro-fessional and correct.

Jennifer studied the course. It looked quite difficult. Would she ever remember which way to go once she was alone in that enormous arena? Suppose her memory deserted her completely? It would be awful to be disqualified for taking the wrong course. She felt dizzy and the plan began to swim before her eyes in the most disconcerting manner.

"Ready, dear? Smith is bringing the pony across—I think you ought to ride her round for a little while."

Jennifer turned in the direction of the speaker, a tall woman in the inevitable grey flannel suit that seemed nowadays to be the Englishwoman's uniform at all sporting events. Her daughter, a thin child with dark plaits, replied peevishly, "All right, don't *fuss*, Mummy. There's lots of time yet."

Competitors were allowed to ride around the outer ring, then, and exercise their mounts. That made her feel a little better, and after collecting her number she went off to get Skipper ready. She gave him a final rub over with a clean cloth, brushed his tail well and picked out his feet. He was now looking very well and smart, his coat gleaming like old mahogany. He looked the part; now what about herself? She pulled a mirror out of the rucksack and propped it up on the manger. Her tie was all crooked and her wig looked a little tousled, so she combed it gingerly and pinned it still more firmly to her head; then, putting on the black velvet hunting cap, she retied her tie, fastening it with the little gold hunting whip that her father had given her, polished her shoes and slipped on her jacket. How thankful she was that the old herringbone had finally grown too tight for her and had had to be discarded in May! Dress was very important at the International.

She slipped a little black-cat mascot into her pocket, and then came the moment when she realised very forcibly that she was really and truly a competitor and not an onlooker—the moment when she tied the string of the number round her waist, and the big black figures 393 labelled her like cattle for slaughter.

Then, collecting her clean gloves and riding stick, she led Skipper out of the box and across to the outer collecting ring.

By the time she arrived quite a lot of children were working their ponies; walking, trotting and cantering around, amid comments and directions from their parents and trainers. There was a pole too, which one or two were jumping over.

"Go on, Miss, 'ave a go," said a bandy-legged little man who was standing by the fence.

Jennifer put the pony straight at it, and as he was taken completely by surprise he hesitated, jumped raggedly and caught the pole behind.

"You canter 'im around a bit first. You didn't give

'im a chance then," said the little man encouragingly. "No need to be nervous now."

His friendly grin reassured her and she followed his advice. As Skipper stood back and hopped over it effortlessly the second time she felt a little more confident, and continued to exercise the pony.

But soon the loneliness came over her again. All the others had so many people fussing around them and encouraging them. It helped a great deal, when you were feeling sick with nervousness, to have someone to talk to. She felt like a wandering waif in an alien land, and bent her head low on her pony's neck, gathering a little comfort from the warm familiar coat.

"'Ere, Miss, ain't you feeling well?"

Jennifer raised her head to see the little man standing looking up at her with an anxious expression. "N-no, I'm quite all right—just a little nervous."

The man pushed his old bowler further back on his head and smiled, his weatherbeaten face creasing into a thousand wrinkles and his eyes alight with a knowing twinkle.

"Oh, we all feel loike that at toimes, but we get used to it. You ain't done much of this afore?"

Jennifer shook her head. "No, not much."

He patted Skipper's neck. "Grand sort of pony you've got; proper little jumper too."

Jennifer smiled. The little man seemed so nice and friendly, and by his worn breeches and brown-gaitered legs she guessed that he knew his way around and had spent all his life with horses.

"W-what time is it?" she queried, more for something to say than anything else, as she had her own watch.

"Nine-forty. Won't be long now. You'll soon be walking the course and seeing from close to, loike, what you've got to pop over."

Jennifer's face crumpled. She had forgotten one of the most vital factors. How could she walk the course when there was no one to hold her pony?

"'Ere, what's the matter now? It ain't that bad, you know."

"It's n-not that, it's——" She looked round wildly. All the other children were dismounting and their ponies were being led away. Now her little man would have to go too, and she would be quite alone again and utterly helpless. Whatever was she going to do?

"Look, Miss," he said, sizing up the situation quickly. "If your folk ain't here yet, I'll 'old the pony while you walks round. I'll be glad to."

"Oh, thank you, thank you so much." Jennifer could have hugged him on the spot. "But haven't you someone else to look after or something?"

"No, not at the moment loike. 'Ere, you'd better be off or else you won't 'ave toime to see it all—and try to get be'ind a good kid and listen to what they're told."

Jennifer walked up the tan-covered passageway to the inner collecting ring. She was in the middle now, looking up, and it was very awe-inspiring.

She recognised the girl ahead of her as Rosemary Perkins, the well-known juvenile rider who had a string of ponies and carried off most of the major awards. She was accompanied by her trainer, a tall man with spindle legs and a slight stoop. Jennifer stuck close behind them, listening attentively to everything he said.

As they came to the trough at the bandstand end of the arena, the man said: "You'll have to use your legs well, as Rocket and Crispin may peek at it, and don't forget you jump this one twice. Then ride well into that corner"—he pointed his stick—"so that you approach fence No. 4 straight. It's a double, and if you cut that corner you'll have the yellow wall down as sure as fate."

She took in all the comments at every fence and realised that the information given was going to help her more than she had realised. The approach to a fence was all-important, and a novice rider in the ring could easily make a mess of it, however good the horse.

The time was drawing very near now, and as the judges entered the ring the bell rang for the competitors to clear the course. The first one was already mounted and walking round the inner collecting ring.

Jennifer went back to find Skipper being led quietly round by the little man.

"Goodness, the fences look enormous when you walk up to them."

"You don't want to take no notice of the 'eight. If you rides smoothly and keeps your 'ead you'll be all right. The great thing to remember for you young 'uns is not to be too clever, but to approach those fences straight, so that your pony can see 'em first. What number do you jump?"

"Number twenty-four."

"That's good. You leave the pony with me and go and 'ave a look at the others going round. It'll help you to remember the course and to see what to do."

"But——" began Jennifer.

"Now you do as I say; no need to worry about me— ain't got anything else to do."

Jennifer did not realise at first that he was quite unattached and was hanging around simply because he could not keep away from a show ground. He had spent his life with show-horses and jumpers, and now he had retired and was living with a married sister near London, he felt completely at a loose end and bored to distraction. To be part of the show world again was like a tonic to him.

After four competitors had been round Jennifer began to worry about Skipper. Was the man looking after him? She ran back, frightened, only to be met by his cheery face and a placid pony walking quietly round.

"'Ow's it going?" he queried.

"All right," replied Jennifer. "There hasn't been a clear round yet; the best so far is four faults. I say, I must tell you. Something very odd happened to one competitor. He was disqualified after jumping the first fence! He didn't touch it either!"

"Ah, I expect 'e forgot to go through the starting tape."

Jennifer looked startled. "Starting tape?"

"Yes," replied the man. "You remember, those white posts."

"The ones you have to go through before the first fence?"

The man nodded. "Well, there's a tape there that sets the clock going—that's 'ow they time them."

"Oh, I see," said Jennifer. "I was wondering how they could get the time accurately with a man pressing a stop watch. But he went through the posts."

"Then 'e started without waiting for a signal from the judge."

"You mean——"

"Yes, Miss, you walk or canter around until you 'ear the starting bell. That's the signal from the judges that they are ready for you. If you goes before that you'll be disqualified."

"Oh dear," sighed Jennifer, "there is so much to remember, Mr.——"

"Barker is the name, Miss," he put in as a great burst of applause came from the stands. "A clear round, I expect. You go back and 'ave another look, it will help you quite a bit. The pony'll be O.K."

Jennifer needed no second bidding. The standard was very high, for few ponies hit more than two fences. As the competition progressed one or two incidents puzzled her. For instance, one girl, after jumping a faultless round, was given two faults. Had she hit a fence that the crowd failed to notice? No, that was impossible, because under F.E.I. Rules a mistake at any fence counted four faults as against the B.S.J.A. Rules where it was two faults for hind legs and four faults for fore-legs. She decided to return and ask Barker.

He smiled. "Was she going very slowly?"

Jennifer nodded. "Yes, quite, and terribly carefully too."

"That explains it then, Miss—she got toime faults. Every second over the time allowed counts a quarter of a fault." He noticed her worried expression. "Remember, Miss, it's better to incur a quarter of a fault than four faults. If you ride with too much thought of the clock you'll like as not rush your fences and have 'em down. There, Miss, they're signalling you in to the inner collecting ring."

Jennifer mounted. "Will you come through with me, Barker?"

The man's face lit up; this was the moment he had been waiting for, the chance to get really inside. He walked at the pony's head, feeling like a king again.

"Number three hundred and twenty-three, disqualified."

"Goodness, whatever for this time?" gasped Jennifer. "It looked like another clear round."

Barker chuckled. "She was so excited at doin' a perfect round that she forgot to go through the finishing post."

If you didn't hit a fence or incur time faults you seemed to get disqualified. There were certainly a great many hazards to the competition. There was no question about it, you had to have your wits about you.

"Now, Miss, listen very carefully," said Barker seriously. "I've found out that there is already five clear rounds, four with time faults and eight with four faults. As there is ten more to jump after you, you may find that in the final they only allows those with clears and time faults in."

"But it says the first eighteen qualify."

"That's as may be, but if they get fourteen with clears and time faults and the next eight have four faults, that makes twenty-two to jump in the afternoon, and they just won't 'ave the time. Ride steady, Miss, and ride for a clear. With time faults you'll qualify, with one fence down you won't"

Jennifer was beginning to feel sick again, and the butterflies in her stomach and the thumping of her heart seemed to completely engulf her.

"Give 'im a canter round now, Miss; only two more before you goes."

Jennifer collected Skipper and cantered round and round mechanically. The pony seemed very calm, not in the least worried or excited.

"Number three nine three."

"Good luck, Miss," whispered Barker. "You can do it."

Those words made Jennifer's heart sing instead of thump, and once she crossed the threshold of the arena all her nervousness seemed to be wafted away as if by magic. She felt very cool, calm and collected as she waited for the bell.

Through the starting post and quietly up to the first fence, a brush and two white poles; Skipper pricked his ears and hopped over. On to the chicken coop, then left-handed and up to the trough. She felt Skipper hesitate, and so used her legs and went on to clear it.

Now the combination fence. She rode right into the corner and approached it straight, for there was only one stride between the oxer and the wall. Next, the gate, which she came up to slowly, as it was a straight fence. Then coming round to the triple bar she put on more speed, and Skipper sailed over it like a bird. Directly after it, she pulled him back on his hocks, for if she galloped on too fast at the brush spread, he might be off his legs. As soon as he was between her hands and

legs again she urged him on, because spread fences
needed speed in order to get the distance. Once over
that she nearly made a fatal mistake. She had even begun
her approach to the trough when she remembered the
brush and logs in the centre, and swinging the pony badly
she pulled left-handed away from it. To help counteract
her mistake she took a rather wide sweep round to the
eighth fence to get the pony going steadily again.

After the trough she cut the corner and approached
the sleepers and gate quite wrong, and for one awful
second she thought the pony was going to refuse. But
he put in a quick one and literally screwed over it, just
touching the top of the fence. The gate wobbled but
did not fall. Lastly, the water, where she sat down and
really rode at it. Skipper responded, and they were over
and through the finishing posts.

Barker was standing by the exit to greet her. "Well
done, Miss, that was a wonderful round. My, that pony
can jump!"

Jennifer slipped to the ground and, patting Skipper,
gave him a sugar lump as a reward.

"Number three nine three. One and a half faults. No
jumping faults, one and a half time faults."

"Have I qualified then?" gasped Jennifer, flushed
with triumph and excitement.

"Yes, I think so," replied Barker, "but we can't be
sure until after the competition. Now, I suggest as you
won't get a prize this morning that we put him back in
'is box, feed 'im, and get 'im ready in case 'e is wanted
this afternoon. If you tell me what number yer box is
I'll do 'im for you, Miss."

"Thank you, Barker, but I'll come too. I feel a bit
wobbly at the knees now."

"Did you eat any breakfast, Miss?"

"Not much," said Jennifer wryly.

"Well, you are going to eat a good lunch right away."

Jennifer smiled. She liked the way the old man had taken over. He knew what he was talking about too, and she was content to take his advice.

She patted Skipper again as they walked away. It was wonderful to know that they had jumped well, and might even have qualified for the championship.

CHAPTER THIRTEEN

"No news yet, Gordon?" Mrs. Charrington, looking pale and wide-eyed, stood framed in the door of the study.

Her husband shook his head. He had been dozing fitfully all night in the leather armchair, his hand resting by the telephone. Mrs. Charrington came in and sank down wearily in the opposite chair, pushing a stray wisp of hair impatiently out of her eyes. "But how can she have disappeared? A girl with hair like hers and riding a pony simply can't vanish into thin air."

"Well, she has," replied Mr. Charrington flatly.

"You read about such terrible things in the papers these days, I feel certain something has happened to Jennifer."

"You're completely disregarding the note she left us, then?"

"But of course," cried Mrs. Charrington impatiently. "She was made to write that, quite obviously."

"You mean, she met someone between here and the Brentwoods'?"

"Yes, I do."

"Well, my dear, it's no use speculating and upsetting yourself even more; we can only wait and see what the police find out. They have their best men on the job. Let me make you a cup of tea—you look all in."

Mrs. Charrington smiled up at her husband; he was being so thoughtful, and a tower of strength.

After he had disappeared into the kitchen she picked up Jennifer's note and kept reading it over and over again. "Do not worry. See you Sunday." Where could the child be? Whatever did it mean? She looked up at the grandfather clock whose deep-throated tick rang out in the same smooth measured way in crises and in happiness. Time moved on relentlessly, even if the heart stood still. It was now six-thirty a.m.; perhaps the morning would bring the long-awaited news. She clenched her hands and offered up a silent prayer.

But the hours crawled by, and though the 'phone pealed through the house it brought nothing but routine messages which all ended in the same hopeful manner. "Don't worry, sir, we'll be on to it soon."

Out on the farm Jenkins was worried, but did not share the same pessimistic view as the others, for he had a feeling that she was up to something, something she had planned herself. When he took the milk up to the house Mrs. Long met him on the doorstep with a cup of tea. "She were always a one, she were. Now if you ask me——"

"Got a paper?" interrupted Jenkins.

"Yes, but there's only a little bit about it—no 'eadlines or nothing like that."

Jenkins threw her a look of scorn. "You women! I didn't want it for that."

"The racing news then, no doubt."

Jenkins did not reply, he was too taken up with his own ideas. There was just a chance that he might be right. He turned over the pages quickly and there on the centre page he saw the answer to his query—the picture of a girl jumping at the White City. He crumpled the paper in his hand and sprang up. "Is Mr. Charrington in?"

"Of course 'e is. Never stirs from the telephone, poor gentleman."

"Well, I'm going through to see 'm."

"Not in them boots you're not."

"Blast the boots!" exploded Jenkins. "I ain't going to see the governor in my stocking feet to please you." He stalked out with dignity, and after picking his way on tiptoe across the polished floor, knocked on the study door.

"Come in. Yes, Jenkins?"

The man stood twisting his cap in his hands. "Sir, might I ring Lady Peebles?"

Mr. Charrington looked more than surprised. "Lady Peebles is on her way over. She should be here any second now. But why the request, Jenkins?"

"W-well, I 'ave an idea, sir, about Miss Jennifer, but I didn't want to say nuthing, not until I'd spoke to 'er ladyship."

"I see."

The doorbell pealed through the house. "That will be Lady Peebles now, I expect." He rose and went out to greet his mother-in-law.

Jenkins, still standing clutching his cap, glanced round the room that smelt faintly of leather upholstery and pipe-tobacco smoke. He noticed the shelves of books, the pictures of aircraft, the flight-engineering books placed neatly beside the farming magazines, the silver model of the Arrowhead in the centre of the big kneehole desk in the window, flanked on one side by a photograph of Mrs. Charrington and on the other by one of Jennifer on Skipper. He advanced and looked at it more closely:

she sat the pony well and even in the picture one could see the determined expression on her little face.

"I'm very annoyed that you didn't let me know about all this before," said Lady Peebles as she entered the room.

"Well, we didn't want to worry you."

"Worry, fiddlesticks. I can stand worry as well as any of you. It would have been much worse if I'd heard the police message on the news."

"Well, you never do listen to the nine o'clock news."

"True, but you never can be sure when an old lady will change her mind. Well, Jenkins," said Lady Pebbles, turning to the man. "You had something to ask me?"

"Yes, m'lady. It's concerning the pony, m'lady. Where did you buy him?"

Lady Peebles lifted her eyebrows. "Really, Jenkins, at a time like this I don't think it has the slightest bearing on the immediate problem."

"Beggin' pardon, m'lady, but I think it 'as. You see, the International 'Orse Show is on in London."

Lady Peebles let out an exclamation. "You think she's gone there?"

The man nodded. "Yes, m'lady. The juvenile jumping is today, and if the pony——"

"The pony's all right—it's registered in my name, Grade J.A."

"Ah, I thought so. I always said it was a top-class pony," muttered Jenkins triumphantly.

"Yes, Jenkins, but Miss Jennifer didn't know that, and to enter for——"

"But she did," exploded Mr. Charrington.

"How?"

"You left the letter stating that very fact open on your table one day when Jennifer was there to tea, and she read it."

"I see." Lady Peebles paused thoughtfully for a moment. "But surely, with half the police in the county looking for her, they would have found her by now if she had gone there."

"You'd have thought so, certainly," replied Mr. Charrington.

"Unless she disguised herself," put in Jenkins.

Lady Peebles looked up sharply. "That's possible, I suppose. How about her friend June Brentwood? Does she know anything?"

"Apparently not. I've spoken to her twice already."

Lady Peebles muttered something under her breath, and after a certain amount of discussion finally persuaded her son-in-law to get June on the telephone.

"Hullo," she said briskly. "Lady Peebles here. Have you any idea where Jennifer is? Has she sworn you to secrecy at all?"

"No, honestly she hasn't."

"She has not told you that she intended to take Skipper to the International Horse Show?"

"No!" gasped June.

Her surprise was genuine enough. The child obviously did not know anything. "Tell me, have you ever seen her jump the pony?"

"Yes, once. She took Skipper round our field when the fences were up to regulation height one day, and he cleared everything. He is *super*!"

"Did she ever mention the International to you?"

"Well, she was always terribly interested in it and

used to ask questions about shows." June stopped suddenly.

"Yes. Yes. Are you there, June?"

"Lady Peebles, I've suddenly remembered something. It was after Jennifer had been to tea—we couldn't find the International Schedule. I remember Daddy searching high and low for it. He wanted to look up something. Oh, Lady Peebles, the jumping is today—do you think that is where she is?"

"Yes," replied the old lady firmly, "I do. Goodbye for the present."

"Well, that's that," said Lady Peebles, as she replaced the receiver. "Jennifer has gone to the White City."

"But you can't be sure."

"As sure as I am of anything. Don't you agree, Jenkins? She's been working very hard with you, hasn't she?"

"Yes, m'lady, and she shows great promise too."

"How do you think she'll get on today?" queried Lady Peebles with a twinkle.

"Well——"

"*Katherine!* If you are so certain we'd better get on to the police straight away and——"

"NO!" thundered the old lady. "We'll go and find out for ourselves. We don't want hordes of police snooping around the Show and upsetting her."

"Upsetting?"

"Yes, upsetting," replied Lady Peebles firmly. "We'll go there and find her ourselves."

Mr. Charrington, puce in the face, was just about to embark on a first-class row when his wife walked slowly in through the door. "Any news yet?" she queried wearily.

"There is, my dear," replied Lady Peebles, rising to her feet. "Jennifer has taken Skipper to the International Horse Show."

Mrs. Charrington stepped back, covering her mouth with her hand. "Oh! Are you sure?"

"Well, I've no proof, if that's what you mean; but, all the same, I know it."

"You mean she is going to jump there?"

"Yes."

"Then get on to the police quickly and stop her. She'll kill herself."

"No she won't, Vanessa. She rides well, Jenkins will tell you that, and the pony is one of the most experienced in the country today." She glanced at her watch. "Anyway, the preliminary is this morning, and as it is now twelve o'clock she will have jumped already."

Mrs. Charrington collapsed in a chair, her face as white as chalk. Everyone was so busy fussing round her that it was several seconds before they noticed Mrs. Long standing grimly in the doorway, holding up a bottle.

"What is it, Mrs. Long?"

"A bottle of 'air dye, Mum. I found it in Miss Jennifer's room."

"I thought so," muttered Jenkins. "She's disguised 'erself. That's why the police ain't found 'er."

"Dyed her hair dark brown! Oh, no!" gasped Mrs. Charrington.

Lady Peebles took the bottle. "Well, she hasn't used any of this. It's quite full. But you're right, Jenkins; she disguised herself somehow, that's certain. Well, what are we waiting for? Let's get off to London," said Lady Peebles, firmly taking charge of the situation.

And as everyone was too exhausted to argue with her they meekly followed her directions. If she was proved wrong they would at least be doing something instead of sitting idly around waiting for the telephone.

"It's after twelve now. If we leave at twelve-thirty we should be there by three o'clock, in time for the afternoon performance."

CHAPTER FOURTEEN

B ARKER was right. Only clear rounds and time faults qualified for the championship. There were fifteen altogether, and Jennifer was one of them. A few people whose children had incurred four faults tried to complain, saying that it stated in the catalogue that the first eighteen would be allowed to jump in the afternoon. But as ten children had got four faults, that meant twenty-five would have to compete, and time did not allow for such a number.

The morning's contest had resulted in two jump-offs before the winner was decided, so the competition was going to be very keen in the championship.

Jennifer obeyed Barker implicitly and went off to lunch at twelve-thirty. Although she literally had to force herself to eat, the butterflies in her stomach being very active, she did manage to get a little down.

When she returned she found that Skipper had eaten very well, and seemed quite unperturbed by the morning's adventures. Barker was strapping him and whistling contentedly through his teeth.

"You look better for that, Miss. You mark my words, it ain't no good trying to do things on an empty stomach."

"I had another look at the plan of the course for this afternoon while I was over there. It's much the same as this morning, except we don't have to jump the bush and logs, and the trough only once. I must remember that," muttered Jennifer to herself. "I shall try and get behind Rosemary Perkins when we walk the course. She won the preliminary, and her trainer's hints certainly helped me no end."

"There's one class this afternoon before the jumping, isn't there?"

"Yes, the final judging of the 14-2 ponies."

"Well, that'll take 'alf an 'our, so I suggest you tidies up now, Miss. I'll get the pony ready and we'll go across, so that you can ride 'im about and get 'im goin'."

When they arrived at the outer collecting ring once again, Jennifer went straight across to the notice-board to see the draw. She could have jumped for joy; she was drawn fifteenth.

"Ah, that's the place to be, Miss. Once the competition 'as started you go through and 'ave a look, like you did last time."

Jennifer had no qualms now about leaving Barker in charge of her precious pony.

"After you've ridden round a bit I'd just pop 'im over the pole once if I was you."

Jennifer nodded. "Right, Barker."

She concentrated on the job in hand and tried to push the coming contest to the back of her mind and control the sinking feeling in the pit of her stomach.

At last the 14-2 ponies came out. The winner, a lovely liver-coloured chestnut with a small girl in a blue riding habit riding side-saddle, looked like an animal out of a dream.

"Them ponies gets better and better each year," said Barker. "There's a lovely mover for you. Look at the way that chestnut throws 'is toe!"

Jennifer nodded. They really did look wonderful, their coats gleaming like satin in the sunlight.

"Well, Miss, time to walk the course. 'Opes you get be'ind that girl again and listens to everything that's said. That trainer of 'ers is a wizard."

Jennifer needed no second bidding; she walked through and, waiting until Rosemary Perkins and the man appeared, followed them once again into the arena, trying to look as if it was the last thing she intended to do.

She looked up and gasped, for instead of a smattering of people in the huge stand there was now a sea of faces stretching up on all sides, tier upon tier of them. The brightly coloured dresses of the women, the fluttering flags, the red carpet and the blue and gold of the Royal Box made an unforgettable kaleidoscope of colour as the notes of the Marine band soared into the air.

This was the White City, the acme of the show world, and she, Jennifer Charrington, was about to compete for one of the most coveted juvenile jumping prizes in England. It seemed almost unbelievable!

The second fence was now a bridge instead of a chicken coop; she would have to take that steadily. But the trough was the greatest surprise of all, for there, floating on the water, were three yellow celluloid ducks, which caused great amusement as they bobbed merrily up and down. The other fences were the same, except that they had been raised three inches, and fences number six and seven had spreads of four feet.

"You will have to increase your speed at these two," remarked the tall man, "as they both are higher and wider." Jennifer listened attentively to all that was said and found the information invaluable.

The bell rang then. The Juvenile Championship had begun.

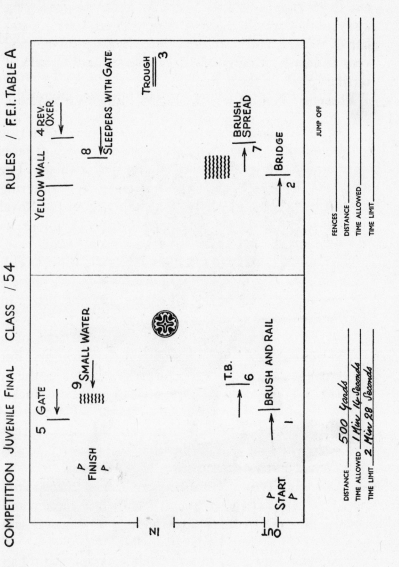

The ducks completely upset everyone's calculations, and the trough proved the tricky fence, the ponies shying away as they caught sight of them. There were a number of refusals and one small boy, whose pony stopped very suddenly, jumped the fence alone, landing with a terrific splash in the water.

Rosemary Perkins was the eighth competitor to jump.

She approached the trough using her legs brilliantly, and, drawing her stick at the last second, she gave the pony a sharp one behind the saddle. It was a case of rider thinking just that split second before the horse. She took all the other jumps well and rode out of the ring amidst a thunder of applause—a clear round.

Jennifer ran back to Barker, who had heard the telltale roar of the crowd. "A clear round?"

Jennifer nodded.

"Well, you'll do the same," he said cheerfully. "Look, they want you in the inner collecting ring. I'll lead him through this time, and you can mount inside."

One girl was disqualified for exceeding the time limit, while the twelfth competitor, a boy on a sturdy grey cob, rode brilliantly, and although he touched the yellow wall and a brick moved to a precarious angle, it did not fall. A lucky clear round.

Two more and then it was her turn. Her heart began to thump again and the palms of her hands were wet; she felt cold in spite of the heat, and shivered.

"Come on, Miss, don't look so worried; get the pony going!"

Jennifer obeyed, then pulled up at the entrance to the ring as the last competitor cleared the water.

She rode in, and once again all nervousness left her.

"Competitor now jumping, No. 393, Miss Katherine Peebles riding Skipper."

The bell rang, the judges were ready. She did not panic but cantered round in a small circle before going through the starting posts. Over the brush and rail and the bridge and round to the trough.

Approaching this, Skipper gathered speed; then seeing the floating objects on the water, he hesitated and

Jennifer thought he was bound to refuse. She used her legs and he seemed to leave the ground all at once, clearing the poles but dropping one hind leg on the edge of the trough, a very awkward performance, and the crowd groaned as they saw a splash of water. Luck was on her side, though, for Skipper was soon balanced again and this enabled her to turn the corner and meet the double fence in the right strides.

The gate seemed a big one, but they were right and cleared it with inches to spare. Over the triple and brush spread and round the trough. She remembered not to jump it again! Skipper put in a short one at the gate and sleepers but cleared it, and as he landed she heard a whisper run through the crowd: "Go on, go on." The hands of the clock must be creeping round fast. She sat down and urged the pony on. He went like a bird and flew the water. The crowd broke into thunderous applause.

"Well done, Miss," said Barker, who was there to greet her as before.

Jennifer dismounted and patted the pony. "We made a mistake at the trough, though, didn't we?"

"No. 393 a clear round."

Jennifer looked at Barker incredulously. "But——"

"No, it were all right, Miss—you didn't 'it the poles; that is the only thing that matters there."

Jennifer breathed a sigh of relief. "Oh, Barker, Barker, isn't it wonderful!"

"It is an' all, Miss. You rode like an old-stager. Your folks should be mighty proud of you."

At the mention of her parents a cloud passed over Jennifer's face. She prayed they were not too worried, and vowed that as soon as the competition was over she would find a telephone box and ring them up.

Had she been able to peep into the stands she would have seen Lady Peebles, her black stick clicking on the concrete steps, leading her mother and father to their seats. The old lady opened her programme and a chuckle escaped her. "Look at that, Vanessa, I told you she was here. No 393, Katherine Peebles, horse Skipper, rider K. Charrington. Quite right—she's entered him in my name. Well, she's got it all worked out, the young monkey."

Mrs. Charrington gasped and half-rose from her seat. Her mother laid a restraining hand on her arm just as the loudspeaker came to life.

"As there are three clear rounds Competitors Nos. 341, 360 and 393 will be required to jump-off for first prize. Fences Nos. 5 and 6 will be raised."

A long sigh emanated from Lady Peebles' clenched lips. "She did it!"

"Mother, I'm going down to stop her."

"You'll do nothing of the sort, Vanessa," snapped the old lady, with a firm tap of her stick. "She has been unpardonably naughty, but to reach this point and then be made to withdraw—no! What do you say, Gordon?"

Mrs. Charrington looking imploringly at her husband, who, glancing first at his mother-in-law and then at the vivid scene before him, was caught in its magic grasp. A showman at heart, he felt a terrific surge of pride for his determined, self-willed daughter. She was made of the stuff pilots were made of.

"She must be allowed to continue now," he said firmly. "We'll have to punish her in some other way."

"But the fences," wailed Mrs. Charrington. "They're enormous!"

"Fiddlesticks! That pony can manage them, and don't forget they fall down."

"That's what Edith Brentwood said and——"

"Ssh!" hissed Lady Peebles. "The first child's coming in to jump. Rosemary Perkins, too. She's good —wins nearly everything."

A hush fell on the crowd. She went round steadily, riding brilliantly at the gate and the trough, and rode out with another clear round to her credit.

The boy went next and was very unlucky to hit the first fence, the lowest one of all.

Then it was Jennifer's turn, and she rode in and cantered round while the well-known clerk of the course, a slim, elderly man with a black bowler tipped over his nose, checked the first fence.

Lady Peebles chuckled again. "That's where the hair dye went! On the pony's legs. Skipper had two white socks."

Mr. Charrington trained his field-glasses on her. "Her hair's black too! She must have had another bottle of dye."

"Those lovely curls! How could she? I can't look, Gordon." Mrs. Charrington closed her eyes tightly and gripped her husband's arm.

The bell rang and Jennifer approached the first fence. Skipper, seeming to understand the importance of the occasion, never looked like putting a foot wrong; he even ignored the bobbing ducks. A clear round. The applause rose like a clap of thunder into the still air.

"Magnificent, magnificent!" cried Lady Peebles. "I knew she could do it! I knew it!"

"I believe you did, Mother. I believe you hoped something like this would happen when you bought the pony!" said Mrs. Charrington, turning her steady blue eyes on her mother with an enquiring look.

"Ah, maybe I did," she replied softly. "What did you think of that, Gordon? Did it make you feel proud of her?"

"It did," he replied solemnly.

"Competitors Nos. 341 and 393 will be required to jump again for first prize. This time it will be over a shortened course over fences Nos. 1, 2, 3, 4 and 5. Fences Nos. 2 and 4 will be raised."

Mrs. Charrington groaned. "I can't bear it! I can't bear it!"

Rosemary Perkins with her chestnut, Rocket, came in for the third time. She approached the double steadily, not realising that the greater the height the greater the speed. She jumped the oxer perfectly; but not having sufficient speed, the pony stood back too far and hit the wall. The crowd groaned. Four faults.

"Good luck, Miss. Now remember, take it steady, but go on at the double."

She patted the pony's neck. "Do your best, Skipper," she whispered. One ear came back by way of an answer.

As she came to the double she remembered Barker's words and Rosemary's mistake. She went on and the extra speed gave her the momentum to get nearer the wall, and so she was able to clear it. Then on and over the last fence with an impudent flick of the heels.

They had done it! She was so excited that she very nearly forgot to go through the finishing posts.

The applause rose and fell like the roar of the sea. Barker, his face purple with excitement, was clapping furiously. "Well done, Miss! Well done!"

Jennifer felt too dazed to reply; she just patted Skipper's neck and swallowed the lump that kept rising into her throat.

"There, Miss," said Barker, leading the pony round, "they're calling you in now. Don't forget to stand out in front of the others when you line up."

Jennifer nodded as she walked slowly back into the big arena. Her fingers tightened on the reins and the crowds seemed to sway and blur before her eyes as she pulled up and turned to face the Royal Box, the others forming up in line behind her.

This was the moment she had dreamed would be hers. This supreme moment which culminated in the realisation of her greatest ambition.

"I'll hold the pony for you while you receive the cup," said a voice beside her.

She glanced down at a man in a grey suit and bowler.

"Thank you," she half-whispered as she watched a small group of people cross the red-carpeted bridge into the ring.

The president of the Show handed the Duchess of Downshire, who was presenting the prizes, a blue rosette, and the next minute a black-gloved hand rested on Skipper's neck.

"Congratulations! You rode very well. What a lovely pony!"

"Thank you," muttered Jennifer shyly as the rosette was clipped to the bridle.

"Now," whispered the man beside her.

She slipped to the ground and suddenly felt her knees wobble. She could not collapse here—it would be too awful! She lifted her head, stuck out her chin and gripped her leather stick as if it was a pillar of stone. They smiled at her, and as she stepped forward to receive the trophy she heard the cameras click.

The great cup glinted in the sun and threw lines of silver magic towards her. She leant forward and took it from the Duchess's outstretched hands. And as her fingers clasped the gleaming surface of the Juvenile Jumping Challenge Cup a tremor of excitement, like a flash of electricity, shot through her being.

Words of congratulation dropped around like rain, and the man in the grey suit took the cup from her as she mounted Skipper once again. She was relieved to find that her knees stopped shaking as soon as they came into contact with the saddle.

"Smile, Miss. That's fine!" said a press photographer.

"How old is your pony?"

"That was an exciting competition."

"How long have you been riding?"

The questions came in staccato fashion, rather like the rattle of a machine-gun, while the Duchess presented the rosettes to the others behind.

"Right, away you go now," said the same calm voice beside her. "Once round the ring."

Skipper pricked his ears and arched his neck, the blue rosette fluttered in the summer breeze, and the applause roared out and up into the sky as they cantered slowly round the ring, at the head of the line.

CHAPTER FIFTEEN

LADY PEEBLES, followed closely by Mr. and Mrs.
Charrington, made her way across to the stables,
her cane clinking triumphantly on the tarmac as
she went.

"But, Mother, even though she *has* won, I still
can't get over what she *did*, running away like that
and——"

"I know, I know; she'll have to be punished, of course.
But it was a superb performance—first time in the ring
too. Quite incredible."

Mrs. Charrington sighed. All the intense anxiety they
had suffered seemed to have vanished from their minds,
for even her husband was bemused with his daughter's
success.

"I'll find the stable manager and get the number of
Skipper's box," said Lady Peebles authoritatively.
"She'll be there, I'm certain."

"To think she managed to arrange all this by
herself," muttered Mr. Charrington. "It's amazing.
I did not think she was capable of getting herself
to London, let alone a pony as well, did you, my
dear?"

Mrs. Charrington shook her head dumbly and walked
along slowly behind them. To think that Jennifer had
taken those enormous fences quite coolly, without any
apparent nervousness, on a pony that not only looked
but performed superbly! The last twenty-four hours

had been so incredible that it left her feeling almost drained of emotion.

Horses looked at her from every side. This was Jennifer's world. She had the courage and the aptitude; it would be no good standing in her way any longer. All parents had at some time or other to swallow the fear they possessed for their children. Mrs. Charrington sighed, and then suddenly stood quite still. Surely that was Jennifer's voice? She advanced and, peering over the stable door, was just in time to see a girl with black bobbed hair sway for a second and then flop back into the arms of a horsey-looking man. As he caught her the black hair slipped and revealed beneath it a mop of fiery-red curls.

"Jennifer, Jennifer," said Mrs. Charrington, struggling with the bolt.

Barker looked first at the child's head and then at the woman in complete bewilderment.

Mrs. Charrington burst into the stable and dropped down beside Jennifer, loosened her tie, and applied cold water to her head and face.

"Fainted from excitement, and no wonder," said Lady Peebles in a matter-of-fact voice.

"W-what happened? Where am I?" mumbled Jennifer as she sat up. "Mummy! Daddy! Gran——"

"Don't talk, dear."

"I'm all right, really. I don't know what happened."

"You felt a little faint, darling."

Jennifer put her hand up to her head, and instead of the straight black hair she felt her own curls—the wig had vanished. Her father smiled. "It slipped as you fell, darling, and Mummy took it off completely."

"Then you know?"

"Yes, we know. We saw you jump."

"You what!"

"We saw you jump *and* win," said Lady Peebles, staring down with pride at the child at her feet. "We arrived just before the jump-off."

"But how did you know——"

"Where to find you?" finished Lady Peebles. "A hunch, my dear, just a hunch."

"Then you're not cross?"

"I wouldn't say that," put in Mr. Charrington. "We are. It was a terrible thing to do."

"But I left a note and told you I was all right and not to worry!"

Mrs. Charrington exclaimed: "Jennifer! Surely you must have realised what we would be thinking. We were absolutely terrified."

"I'm awfully sorry, Mummy, honestly I am."

"We'll go into all that later," said Mr. Charrington firmly. "Of course, you'll have to be punished, and severely too, but I think you've had about enough for one day. And I would like you to know," he added softly, "that we are very proud of you."

"Yes," said Lady Peebles. "You rode magnificently, and used your head."

"Not my head, Granny, Barker's."

"Barker?"

"Yes." She turned to the man who was doing the pony. "He took me under his wing and told me everything."

"Is this true?"

"Well, she looked a little lonely loike, and me being used to shows and all, although I've retired now, as you might say, I thought I'd see if I could 'elp."

"Which you did very successfully," added Lady Peebles. "How do you feel now, dear?"

"Fine, Granny," replied Jennifer, scrambling to her feet.

"I think she'd be all the better for a good meal, if you don't mind my saying so," put in Barker firmly. "She says she 'as eaten all right, but I 'ave me doubts with all this 'ere excitement."

Lady Peebles smiled. "So have I. That's a very good idea. We'll all go across and have tea and watch the *Daily Mail* Cup."

"Granny, could we really? Oh, but what about Skipper; will he——"

"I'll look after 'im, Miss."

"But I've got to get him home and everything."

Mr. Charrington went across to talk to Barker for a few minutes and then, turning to his daughter, said, "You needn't worry about that, darling. Barker is going to look after him and box him home for us." Mr. Charrington drew out his notecase and handed the man ten pounds. "Thank you for keeping an eye on that wayward daughter of mine. See you at the farm to-morrow, then."

"Yes, sir."

Jennifer went across to the pony and put an arm round his neck. "Oh, Skipper, you were wonderful, just wonderful." She turned to her mother. "You won't be nervous of my jumping now, will you?"

Mrs. Charrington hesitated for a brief second; then, catching her husband's eyes, she replied: "Not so much, darling, certainly."

"Oh, good. Did you hear that, Skipper?"

One ear came back and he turned his head round to look at her.

"I believe he knows everything one says and everything that's going on. I know he understood today, he tried so hard."

"And succeeded. Now come along or we shall miss the rest of the programme."

As they walked out of the box ahead of her, Jennifer turned to Barker with a smile. "Thank you so very much for helping me. I could never have done it without the training I had from Jenkins first, and the advice you gave me today. Or without you, of course," she added, planting a kiss on Skipper's velvety nose.

The old man smiled. "Don't you worry about the pony, Miss. I'll bring him back safe and sound. 'E'll be fine with me."

"I know he will," replied Jennifer.

Then, joining her family outside, she slipped her hand into her grandmother's and whispered: "Doesn't the International simply get you, and aren't horses the most wonderful things in the world?"